The helicopter was completely out of control

Dr. Mohammedkhani was not going to be terminated, nor even arrested. She would unknowingly do her job and make sure the upcoming launch went off perfectly.

Dr. Seth was the enemy. Bolan suspected he was not who he pretended to be. The Bear was right. There had been no modifications to the rocket nor any special reentry vehicle built. The weapon was the satellite itself. It would fall with much less accuracy than a guided rocket—but even if it missed Washington completely, some part of the U.S. eastern seaboard would be turned into a radioactive wasteland.

Nothing was going to interfere with the upcoming launch.

Bolan knew that he was about to die in a tragic helicopter accident.

MACK BOLAN ®
The Executioner

The Executioner®
Don Pendleton's

LETHAL
PAYLOAD

A GOLD EAGLE BOOK FROM
W★RLDWIDE.®

TORONTO • NEW YORK • LONDON
AMSTERDAM • PARIS • SYDNEY • HAMBURG
STOCKHOLM • ATHENS • TOKYO • MILAN
MADRID • WARSAW • BUDAPEST • AUCKLAND

First edition January 2005
ISBN 0-373-64314-4

Special thanks and acknowledgment to
Charles Rogers for his contribution to this work.

LETHAL PAYLOAD

Honor et Fidelite (Honor and Fidelity)
Legio Pastria Nosta (The Legion Is My Home)
—Motto of the French Foreign Legion

A solider who betrays his comrades is the worst
kind of traitor. He will have no honor when he
faces his Executioner.

—Mack Bolan

THE
MACK BOLAN®
LEGEND

Nothing less than a war could have fashioned the destiny of the man called Mack Bolan. Bolan earned the Executioner title in the jungle hell of Vietnam.

But this soldier also wore another name—Sergeant Mercy. He was so tagged because of the compassion he showed to wounded comrades-in-arms and Vietnamese civilians.

Mack Bolan's second tour of duty ended prematurely when he was given emergency leave to return home and bury his family, victims of the Mob. Then he declared a one-man war against the Mafia.

He confronted the Families head-on from coast to coast, and soon a hope of victory began to appear. But Bolan had broken society's every rule. That same society started gunning for this elusive warrior—to no avail.

So Bolan was offered amnesty to work within the system against terrorism. This time, as an employee of Uncle Sam, Bolan became Colonel John Phoenix. With a command center at Stony Man Farm in Virginia, he and his new allies—Able Team and Phoenix Force—waged relentless war on a new adversary: the KGB.

But when his one true love, April Rose, died at the hands of the Soviet terror machine, Bolan severed all ties with Establishment authority.

Now, after a lengthy lone-wolf struggle and much soul-searching, the Executioner has agreed to enter an "arm's-length" alliance with his government once more, reserving the right to pursue personal missions in his Everlasting War.

1

"Death to the United States!"

The words were spoken in Arabic, but the Executioner had heard them before, all too often. They were being chanted in such an orgiastic frenzy that Mack Bolan could hear them clearly on the lagoon. Drums and other percussive instruments beat in rhythm to the thundering chant.

"Death to the United States!"

Bolan's canoe slid through the rollers and crunched to a halt in the sand. He stepped into the foam of the Java Sea and dragged the outrigger out of the surf and onto land. The beach was a patchwork of grays, greens and blacks in his night-vision goggles. The chants grew louder and even more excited. There was exultation in the voices of the chanters, and beneath that, expectation. A clear baritone called out and was met by at least thirty voices in answer.

"Death to the United States!"

The call and response grew more and more savage. Bolan smiled grimly. The *pandekar* was in fine form.

"Death to the Great Satan!" a new voice shouted.

Bolan shook his head. The mullah was not willing to be outdone.

The Executioner was wary of rescue missions. They threw every single advantage into the hands of his opponents. He was always outnumbered, always outgunned, and savvy enemies always had multiple opportunities to kill their captives or use them as shields. Bolan, himself, was always in dire risk of killing those he had come to save. The fact was that in the past two years hostage rescues in the Pacific had not all gone according to plan. American and Australian rescue missions in the Philippines and Indonesia had resulted in dead hostages. It seemed as if fate dealt from the bottom of the deck and gave all the high cards to the goblins. It was the same old situation. Bolan was one man, and he held but a single card.

In special operations circles it was spoken of with awe. It was known as surprise. It trumped everything, and there was nothing sweeter when it was achieved.

The chanting from beyond the tree line degenerated into wordless howls and screams of rage. Bolan wasted no time as he marched up the beach.

The voice of the *pandekar* boomed forth. *Pandekars* were master teachers of pentjak-silat, the national martial arts of the Indonesian archipelago. Along with the great technical skills they developed, they were renowned spiritualists, famed for their supernatural powers, rumored to include telepathy, mystic healing and clairvoyance. They were thought to be invulnerable.

Pandekar Binpadgar Regog was a master of the Jokuk style, and was considered by his followers to be a mystic. When the Taliban mullah Abu-Hamid al-Juwanyi had fled Afghanistan during Operation Anaconda, Regog had welcomed the refugee mullah as a divine sign. Al-Juwanyi's teachings of jihad against the

United States had been welcomed and were taken on
with religious fervor by Regog and his followers.

Suddenly a woman's scream cut across the chanting.
Bolan moved quickly through the thin jungle. A two-
story hut dominated the clearing. A number of smaller
huts arced out on either side of the big house in a horse-
shoe shape. A bonfire burned in the middle.

Beside the pyre a pair of posts had been sunk in the
soil and Famke Ryssemus was strung between them.
She was a famous European fashion model who came
to Java annually to help her uncle with his missionary
work. That was enough to make her a target of the *pandekar*. Bolan could see she was bruised and her blond
hair was disheveled, but there was no obvious blood or
serious wounds yet.

The real fun was clearly about to begin.

A half-naked man leaped into the sand near Ryssemus and shrieked. He wore only a red turban, and a
white breechclout tied with a red sash around his hips.
Foam flecked his lips. His wiry musculature stood out
in high relief as his hips and shoulders jerked with the
drumbeats. He tossed away his AK-47 rifle. The cries
of the mob rose as he reached both hands into his sash
and withdrew two Javanese kris. The sinuous handles
of the daggers were carved into the shapes of dragons.
The mob moaned expectantly as he reversed the twelve-
inch undulating blades in his hands. His eyes glazed
over as he aimed the quicksilver weapons at his chest.
Sweat streamed down his torso in rivers. Spittle flew
as he let out a horrific groan. It was matched by the cap-
tive woman's scream of horror as he stabbed both
blades into his own chest.

The crowd roared.

Roughly forty people formed a circle around the fire. Regog and Al-Juwanyi sat on raised divans. A half-dozen men sat cross-legged in the sand at their feet pounding drums and cymbals. The rest of the gathering stood swaying to the music and chanting. All carried bladed weapons, and most also clutched rifles, pistols, or submachine guns. Many in the throng were working themselves into a trance like that of the dancer. They called out wordlessly as the dancer stabbed himself again. The blades stuck between his ribs, and he yanked them forth with a howl.

No blood ran down the dancer's sides.

A man in a trance was said to be unstoppable. Bolan had faced opponents armed with mystical powers on more than one occasion. Around the globe, martial artists and mystics used rigorous training, ritual and special breathing techniques to manipulate their personal energy and aspects of the autonomous nervous system that were on autopilot in most humans. Such people were capable of almost inhuman feats. But most mystical fighting had been rendered obsolete in a modern world of high-capacity automatic rifles and helicopter gunships. Bolan did not believe in magic, but he had long ago learned not to sneer at sorcerers.

Facing such opponents made his one-man rescue operation just a little more nightmarish.

Bolan considered the M-16 he held. If he opened up with his rifle, the mob would blindly, suicidally rush him and he would fall beneath their knives before he managed to empty his magazine, much less reload. However, Bolan had other ideas.

The dancer turned on Ryssemus. She screamed as the man raised his knives overhead like ice picks.

Bolan reached beneath his rifle and slipped his finger around the trigger of the FN 303 Less Lethal Launcher mounted under the forestock. He flicked off the safety, and his thumb pressed down. The laser sight came to life and put a red spot on the knife-wielding dancer's chest.

It was time to see exactly how much control of his autonomous nervous system the dancer really had.

The FN 303 was a glorified paint-ball gun that fired fin-stabilized .68-caliber projectiles. They hit the target like a fist, and breaking on contact to prevent penetration injuries. They were unlikely to stop a highly trained martial artist, much less one in self-induced trance.

But Bolan's rounds had been custom loaded to rather unique specifications.

The Executioner squeezed the trigger three times in rapid succession. The sound of the compressed air launcher was lost in the roar of the chanting and the drums. The dancer stopped at the impacts but did not fall. For a second his glazed eyes narrowed as he searched the crowd for his attacker.

No one in the mob even noticed.

But the chanting faltered as the dancer's legs suddenly wobbled and his knives fell from his hands. The music subsided as the dancer staggered. He took three rapid steps toward his master, then fell clutching his belly. Shouts of indignation replaced the music and chanting as the dancer vomited all over the *pandekar*.

Bolan's projectiles were rear-loaded with Adamsite.

Adamsite had another more colloquial nickname. It was known as vomit gas.

The dancer collapsed in the *pandekar's* lap, convulsing violently.

Bolan began squeezing the trigger of the launcher repeatedly as he moved the laser sight from target to target. The projectiles carried only small loads of the irritant, but as the stunned Javanese milled and tried to help one another, the effects spread like wildfire. The soldier swiftly loaded another 15-round cassette of projectiles and resumed firing. Total surprise had been achieved. The entire mob was down or in the process of falling prey to the Adamsite.

Famke Ryssemus screamed and strained against her bonds. She was seemingly surrounded by a ten-foot halo in the sand. Everyone outside the circle Bolan had drawn lay in their own personal, intestinal hell, part of the greater sea of writhing fanatics. But Bolan could not hold off an army with Adamsite. He had to get in and get out. There were others on the island, and it was only a matter of seconds before the situation would turn deadly.

Bolan pulled on his gas mask and strode out of the trees.

A screaming man staggered into Bolan's path brandishing a razor sharp panga. Tears streamed down his cheeks as he raised the heavy knife over his head. The soldier put a .68-caliber projectile point-blank into the side of the man's neck, and he collapsed unconscious on the sand.

Bolan moved into the circle.

He turned and scooped up a fallen knife. Ryssemus screamed and then collapsed into his arms as he cut her bonds. The soldier leaned toward her ear and shouted through his gas mask. "Close your eyes! Hold your breath!" He lifted her over his shoulder and picked his way back through the heaving throng in the sand. He cleared the gas area and yanked up his mask as he set the woman down.

"Are you all right?" he asked.

She swayed on her feet. Her beautiful blue eyes were as wide as dinner plates. She looked at Bolan like a deer in the headlights of an oncoming truck. "I…"

"Where's your uncle?"

"My uncle?" Miss Ryssemus jolted into awareness. "They tortured him! Oh, my God! He's still in the big hut!"

Bolan took the woman's wrist and pulled her into the trees outside the semicircle of huts. She stared in dull horror as he drew his Beretta 93-R and shoved it into her hands. "Stay here," Bolan said as he flicked the selector to semiauto. "Hold the gun in both hands. Point it and pull the trigger on anyone besides me or your uncle. I'll be right back."

Bolan shoved her down into the bushes and ran through the trees. He skirted the outer perimeter of the horseshoe-shaped village and made for the rear of the biggest hut, which was built on a raised platform of logs. The beams of the structure were solid, but the walls were made of densely woven lengths of split bamboo. Three men with rifles spilled out of the hut and ran down the steps toward the fallen mob. Bolan stayed in the shadows. He crept around the building and stopped at the edge of the veranda.

A man stood with his rifle shouldered, watching the other men run to the circle of writhing bodies. Bolan watched, as well. The men ran and knelt beside their stricken comrades. Within seconds they were doubled over, contorting with nausea.

The man on the veranda stayed put, tracking his rifle

for a target. Suddenly the man turned toward Bolan.
The laser sight of the Executioner's weapon system put
a red dot on the rifleman's head. The silenced M-16
coughed once, and the gunman fell.

Bolan vaulted onto the veranda, but he stopped at
the door.

Every instinct screamed danger.

From within the hut a voice spoke in Dutch, a language Bolan had some understanding of but could not
easily speak. He kept his body behind the heavy teak
beam framing the doorway as he spoke slowly in English.

"Let Pieter Ryssemus go, now, and I will let you
live."

There was a lengthy pause before the answer came
back in very thick English. "Preacher man gonna die,
GI. Throw down your gun. My boy come pick it up, and
maybe we talk."

Bolan drew the 9 mm Centennial hammerless revolver from his ankle holster and tucked it into the back
of his belt. He pulled his pant leg back over the empty
holster and stood. He tossed the assault rifle through the
door. It fell with a clatter.

"All right," the voice beckoned.

Bolan stepped into the doorway.

The hut was a meeting place. The vast majority of
the floor was woven grass matting where people sat and
received instruction. A small, elevated platform near the
back with a pair of cushions marked where the *pandekar* and the mullah held court.

A section of the matting was pulled away, revealing
a hatch in the floor that led to a cellar. A Javanese man
stood in the stairway leading down. He wore a red tur-

ban, and was bare chested and heavily muscled. He held an AK-74 rifle with the buttstock folded and the bayonet fixed. Bolan assessed the situation. The man was an amateur, but he was armed with an automatic rifle and the range was five meters.

The man stared at Bolan's weapon where it lay and then at the empty holster on Bolan's thigh. "Pistol, asshole."

Bolan kept his hands open and down by his hips. "I gave it to Famke."

The man sneered and stepped out of the stairwell. "Where are your Australian SAS friends?"

Bolan had immense respect for the Australian SAS, but they were on the Indian Ocean side of Java and had chosen the wrong island. When Bolan's intel told him where the bad guys were, he hadn't had time to wait.

"I'm alone," Bolan said.

The man shook his head in disgust. "American cowboy asshole."

Bolan remained silent.

The man gave Bolan's weapon system an appreciative look and kicked it into a far corner of the room.

In a split second Bolan's hand was behind his back. He twisted and shoved the snub-nosed Smith & Wesson forward in a fencer's lunge. The kidnapper raised his rifle, but Bolan was already in motion. He aimed and squeezed the trigger.

The gunman's head snapped back as if he had taken a hard jab to the jaw. His knees buckled, and he collapsed onto the matting.

"Diwangkara!" a voice shouted from the cellar. The voice rose in urgency. "Diwangkara!"

"Diwangkara's dead," Bolan said as he crossed the

matting and reclaimed his rifle. He crouched by the hatchway. "And so are you, unless Pieter Ryssemus walks up those stairs now."

"Preacherman injured," was the reply.

"So carry him." Bolan put a fresh magazine into the carbine and racked the action. "Like your life depended on it."

Bolan took a fragmentation grenade from his belt and pulled the pin. He retained the grenade with his fingers clamped on the cotter lever. He tossed the pin down the stairs and listened to it clink on the steps. He took a moment to let that sink in downstairs. "Dutch Intelligence and the Australians want the missionaries." Bolan let that sink in for a moment, as well. "You come up right now and bring Pieter Ryssemus with you, alive, or you'll join Diwangkara."

Waiting for the response, Bolan monitored the noises outside. Adamsite was a persistent gas, and its effects lasted for hours, but the island was several kilometers in diameter, and he by no means had control of it.

"I come up," the man in the cellar said.

"Do it slow."

The timbers of the stairs creaked.

Pieter Ryssemus appeared in the hatchway. Bolan stayed stone-faced as the missionary staggered up the steps. He was a tall man, but his upper body listed in an ugly fashion from a broken collarbone. He was missing several fingers, and his body was covered with burns, bruises and wounds. The missionary had been tortured, not by professional interrogators or even amateurs wanting information. He had been tortured by those who had given in to their hatred. They had tortured the old man for the pleasure it had given them.

There was a Swedish Carl Gustav submachine gun pressed to the old man's temple. The kidnapper stood behind the Dutchman, using his prisoner as a shield. He held Ryssemus's injured arm cruelly twisted behind his back. Most of the terrorist was hidden behind the missionary's body. His eyes glared over the top of his weapon, and he wore a red turban like the rest of his sect. Tattoos crawled up the corded muscles of his forearms. Ryssemus flinched as the gun muzzle was rammed even harder into his skull. The terrorist smiled and revealed missing teeth.

"Drop your gun, GI."

The laser sight on Bolan's carbine clicked on with pressure from his hand, and a red dot appeared just below the kidnapper's turban.

"Drop yours," Bolan replied.

The man's hand whitened on the grip of the submachine gun. "Drop your gun!" he screamed.

Bolan frowned and lowered his rifle slightly.

The terrorist grinned. He did not notice the red laser dot came to rest on his gun hand. "Now, GI, you—"

Brass sprayed as the action of Bolan's carbine clicked. The Swedish submachine gun fell from the shredded remnants of the terrorist's hand. Ryssemus fell from his grip as the kidnapper's eyes widened in horror at the sight of his wound.

The expression became his death mask as Bolan put a 3-round burst through his chest.

The kidnapper tumbled down the stairwell. Pieter Ryssemus collapsed on the floor. Bolan moved swiftly down the stairs. The terrorist lay sprawled in the lower chamber. Bloodstains on the floor and the fetid air of human suffering attested to what the lower room had been used for. Bolan found the pin from his grenade and replaced it. He scanned the room swiftly and took several maps, documents and a cell phone. He knelt beside the dead man and peered at his arm intently. Among the writhing tribal tattoos was a distinctive shield. An Asiatic dragon coiled across the background. Superimposed over the dragon was a very western looking cartoon owl. Above the owl was a tiny, stylized parachute canopy.

The dead man was also wearing dog tags.

Bolan memorized the tattoo. He snapped the dog tags from around the man's neck and took the knife that was sheathed in his sash.

The soldier went back up the stairs. The old man groaned. "Famke?"

"She's safe. She's waiting for us." Bolan surveyed the missionary grimly. He was in bad shape. "Sir, can you walk?"

"I prayed to God for salvation, and you came." He clasped Bolan with his good arm and struggled to rise. Bolan had to do most of the work to get Ryssemus on his feet, but the old man steadied himself and nodded. "But God also helps those who help themselves, and I will walk from this place." The ghost of a smile passed over Pieter Ryssemus's mashed lips. "But I do not know if I can run." He looked down at the submachine gun on the floor. "Swedish."

Bolan scooped up the weapon. "Can you shoot?"

"I was a soldier in the army before I became a soldier of God." The missionary slung the weapon over his good shoulder and took the grip in his hand. He looked back down the stairs at his torturer. "And we are among men who have fallen from the grace of any God I know.

I will pray for their souls." The smile ghosted back across the old man's face. "But later."

Bolan nodded. Missionary life was hard. They often went where disease, poverty and human suffering were at their absolute worst. The Executioner had only to look in the old man's eyes to know he was about as tough as they came.

The soldier clicked on his radio. "This is Striker. I have the package. I am extracting."

Ryssemus raised a hopeful eyebrow. "Helicopters are coming?"

"I have a canoe."

The old man blinked.

Bolan smiled. "Come on. We have a submarine to catch."

2

Stony Man Farm, Virginia

"Well, you're the hero of the hour." Aaron "The Bear" Kurtzman said, "That was about as slick a rescue op as has ever been done. One for the textbooks." Kurtzman made a show of cringing in disgust and waving his hands. "An Adamsite gun, ugh! Gives me the heebie-jeebies just thinking about it. The Cowboy is a sick man."

Bolan stared into the distance, distracted.

Kurtzman grinned hopefully. "I hear a certain super-model was suitably grateful."

Bolan frowned slightly but not at Kurtzman.

The computer expert sighed. "What's bothering you?"

The soldier glanced at the sketch he had made. "What'd you make of the tattoo and the dog tags?"

"A little, why?"

"That guy was in command."

Kurtzman cocked his head. "What about Regog and Al-Juwanyi?"

"It was their show," Bolan agreed. "But the guy in the cellar was in command, at least tactically, and he wasn't part of the ceremony. He was wearing a red turban. He was Javanese. He may have been Muslim, and he was definitely more than just another member of the *pandekar*'s sect.

"Really?" Kurtzman's interest was piqued. "How so?"

"I don't know." Bolan shook his head slowly. "His vibe. He didn't act like some fanatic on guard duty who was missing out on the show of a lifetime. He was way too cool. If he was part of the congregation, he should have come up out of the cellar in berserker mode, foaming at the mouth with two feet of steel in each hand. Instead, he starts making like an FBI negotiator. I don't think the riflemen he sent out were part of the party, either. I wish I'd had time to check them out."

Bolan sat back in his chair. "What'd you get on the sketch I gave you and the dog tags?"

The Bear held up the tags. "These were simple enough. We've got his name, Pak Widjihartani, and his serial number, which implies to me that he at least made sergeant."

"You think he's Indonesian army?"

Kurtzman put down the tags. "I would, except that at the top of the tags are the letters *LE*."

Bolan raised an eyebrow.

The computer expert grinned. "Légion Étrangère."

Bolan raised his other eyebrow. "You think our boy is French foreign legion?"

"I'm betting he was. I'm running what I can on his dog tags now, but I don't think I can get much without actually trying to break into Legion records, and I'd like to try and go the legitimate route first. We do not want to officially piss off the French foreign legion." Kurtzman let out a long breath. "But I doubt very much your pal was acting in any official Legion capacity when you met him."

Bolan was forced to agree, but something about the scenario still bothered him. "How about the tattoo?"

"I don't know." Kurtzman grunted noncommittally. "Some kind of insignia? I couldn't find anything exactly like it in any open military databases, but soldiers have been giving themselves unofficial unit or specific mission patches and insignia since the French and Indian wars. If this is a legion insignia, I bet it's an unofficial one, and not tolerated on formal uniform dress. I suspect it's a custom job. Probably has to do with his company's special role or a mission." Kurtzman sighed again. "Assuming of course that he didn't have it done when he was in the Indonesian army and then joined the legion later. A fair number of legionnaires are veterans of other services. I'm running a check to see if his name or the insignia pops up on any Indonesian or Asian military database we have, but so far we haven't turned up anything. Of course, people who join the legion are allowed to change their names, and often do, so the one on the tag may not be the one his daddy gave him."

"Any other good news?"

"Yeah." Kurtzman grinned lopsidedly. "It's a tattoo. He could have made the damn thing up when he was drunk."

"Bear," Bolan said, sighing wearily, "what would you make of it?"

"All right. Best guess." He peered at the sketch again. "The dragon could mean anything, though if I had to bet, it probably has something to do with service in

Asia. The owl might mean some kind of night operations. It's a specialization in the legion. The parachute's
a no-brainer. Your boy was airborne, and in the French
foreign legion, the paratroops are the elite."

Kurtzman wasn't telling Bolan much he didn't already know, but he was confirming his suspicions. The
computer wizard stared at the sketch again. "These
guys could be mercs. It's not unknown for guys to get
out of the foreign legion and go to work for someone
else. 'Legionnaire' certainly has some prestige attached
to it. Maybe the mullah felt that he needed some extra
muscle with the United States and Australia hunting
him."

Bolan had considered that. "He already had an island
full of muscle with the *pandekar* and his boys. Both
men were also very religious. Al-Juwanyi is Taliban and
Regog is part of the al Qaeda cell network in Indonesia. Neither organization is known for hiring outsiders.
These guys are definitely part of the puzzle."

"Okay, but making them fit isn't going to be fun."

Bolan was all too aware of that. He trusted his instincts, but there were no facts to back them up or leads
to take them anywhere. "What about the cell phone
and the documents I collected on the island?"

Kurtzman clicked a few keys on his keyboard. The
monitor showed Carmen Delahunt rapidly pounding
the keyboard at her workstation. She looked up and
blew a lock of red hair away from her eyes. "What's up,
Aaron?"

"Striker is here, and he's hoping for some answers.
Got any?"

She punched up information. "The cell phone's
memory had some numbers in it. Several were to Ja-

karta, and not surprisingly, they were to phones that were stolen. One led to Bali, and again, dead-ended to a stolen phone. One anomaly was a number that led to French Guiana, which, as you can guess, dead-ended."

"The French foreign legion has its Jungle Warfare School in French Guiana," Bolan said. "Bear, I want a country study, now."

Kurtzman began tapping keys, and a map of South America popped up on his screen. Information began scrolling. They read an encyclopedia-like description of the French colony.

Bolan stared hard at the map inset on the screen. "What kind of transnational issues are we looking at?"

"Very few. They're always asking for increasing autonomy from France, but in public votes only a small percentage of the population supports seceding from France, and they're not a violent faction. Their neighbor, Suriname, claims a strip of their territory between the River Litani and the River Marouini, but it's never come to a military struggle. There is limited illicit marijuana growing along the coast, but that's mostly for local consumption. Interpol considers them to be a minor drug transshipment point to Europe at best. Unemployment is a problem, but not monumental."

"What's the Muslim population?"

Kurtzman could see where Bolan was going. "Miniscule, not enough to register in official population charts. French Guiana is overwhelmingly Roman Catholic. The Muslim community are immigrants, and most likely to be businessmen or university-educated professionals working for French companies." The computer expert's brow furrowed in thought, and he hit more keys. His map tracked westward and information scrolled. "Suriname, however, does have a significant Muslim population."

"From Java," Bolan concluded.

Kurtzman hit a key triumphantly. "Bingo. Suriname was a former Dutch colony, just like Indonesia, and the Dutch imported a lot of Javanese for labor." He lost some of his exuberance. "But that still doesn't get us anywhere. The Javanese are in Suriname, and there are almost none to speak of in French Guiana. It's a non-issue."

"But our boy had a contact there."

"He called a phone number there. They're two tiny countries on the northern tip of South America, and it's a small world."

"Our boy was al Qaeda." Bolan shook his head. "They don't do anything small. He was on a mission, a high profile kidnapping and murder, and he had presets in his cell phone. Those would all be important contact numbers. One of them was in French Guiana."

"Well, it is intriguing, I'll grant you." Kurtzman leaned back in his wheelchair and laced his fingers behind his head. "But how you're going to string this all together into anything significant is beyond me."

"I'm not." Bolan leaned back and matched his comrade's posture. "You are."

"You know, I knew you were going to say that." Kurtzman sat straight up. "How do you want to play it?"

"Suriname has a significant Muslim population, predominantly Javanese, and Regog was a Jokuk stylist, heavy into religion and mysticism, and now it looks like at least some splinter sect of it has gone militant. Do whatever you have to to find any practice of Jokuk-style pentjak-silat in Suriname. Find a connection, no matter how tenuous, and then make it lead to French Guiana."

"All right." Kurtzman chewed his lower lip in thought. "But this is getting thin, sniper. I trust you, and I trust your instincts, but we are officially grasping at straws."

"I know," Bolan said. "But I trust you, Bear. I trust your instincts, and you've worked with a lot less."

Kurtzman laughed. "You keep talking like that, and you're gonna have a date for the prom."

Bolan smiled. "Here's the part where you lose that lovin' feeling."

Kurtzman read Bolan's mind. "You want Akira and me to hack the French foreign legion's military records."

Bolan nodded once. "Yeah."

"Striker, if you're accepted into the legion and want to change your identity and get away from your past, they do everything in their power to help you. This is the kind of info they're going to keep protected. You know what kind of a stink it's going to raise if we get detected breaking into their military databases?"

"So don't get detected," Bolan replied.

"Jeez, Striker, hacking France is—"

"Keep it real mission specific. Find Pak Widjihartani if you can, and any other aliases he may have. Find out where's he's from and where he's been. If he was a legionnaire, find out what regiment he served in and where. Other than that specific info, no sight-seeing. Don't download anything else France or the legion would find sensitive, but I have got to have Pak."

"All right." Kurtzman considered the enormity of the task before him. "I'll lay out a battle plan for Akira and pull up our French translator programs. I can't even begin to imagine what kind of operating systems and safeguards the French foreign legion is using, but I'll start on the assumption it's using the same protection of information protocols as the regular French military. I'll have Carmen download and collate every useful piece of information on the legion that she can find and get a copy made for us. The legion is one of the most colorful military units in the history of mankind, and it should make interesting reading on the plane."

Kurtzman's eyebrow rose once more. "I'm assuming you're getting on a plane."

"Yeah." Bolan yawned and nodded. "But I need a nap. I'm gonna take twenty-four hours' downtime. Then I want to meet with you again to see what we have. Assuming it's anything, I'll need Barbara to arrange a flight to Suriname. I'll need an updated passport and a French visa, and get me a full warload delivered to the U.S. Embassy down there."

"I'm on it."

"Okay." Bolan rose. "I'm sacking out. As soon as you have that information package on the legion, call me."

"One thing, Striker."

"What's that?"

"You be careful about messing in legion business. They have a reputation for killing people who mess with them."

"I've heard that."

3

Paramaribo, Suriname

Bolan removed the bandage and surveyed the handiwork on his arm. It would have to do.

Sweat stung his arm as he stepped out from the air-conditioned hotel, and his shirt soaked through from the ninety-degree heat and the matching humidity. Suriname sat at the top of South America less than two hundred kilometers from the equator. As a nation, Suriname consisted almost totally of its coastal strip; and once one strolled half a kilometer from the surf and sand, the sea breeze ended and the cloistered heat of the tropical rainforest began. The capital city followed the geography. The Europeans clung to the coast. Modern European Dutch-style businesses and homes clustered along the beaches and the waterfronts of the capital. Once one went inland, the tin shacks of the ever-growing ghettos clawed space out of the jungle.

Bolan put the blissful breeze of the sea to his back and walked into the blast furnace.

He was walking into a part of the capital that most people avoided after dark, and where police went only when heavily armed and in number.

Bolan got the directions from the U.S. Embassy, but he could have followed his nose. It was evening, and with the setting of the sun the act of cooking had become tolerable. Bolan walked the invisible borders of the shantytowns by scent and turned to follow the aroma of jasmine rice, curry and simmering coconut milk to the Javanese quarter.

Bolan had few illusions. He was barely armed, and his ruse was as thin as hell. He would not be able to withstand more than a few moments of scrutiny, and if it came to a fight he would never live to reload the little .22 Walther PPK/S tucked in the small of his back. The knife tucked in his boot would be of even less use against men who had spent their entire lives practicing the dances of death with foot-long kris knives and parangs.

People sat outside on the stoops and rattan chairs, taking their ease, or leaned out the windows to try to catch some hint of the evening breeze. They smoked cigarettes and looked sidelong at Bolan with undisguised suspicion as he passed.

Bolan consulted his mental map and approached the practice hall of Pandekar Ali Soerho.

Soerho was a *pandekar* of high repute, of the Jokuk style, from the same lineage as Regog. In this confrontation, Bolan would not have tactical surprise or Adamsite gas to back him up against this mystic warrior and his circle.

The hall was a WWII-vintage Quonset hut that had been repaired many times. Tin siding had been used to patch the walls and the roof. Woven rattan screens covered the windows. The scent of sandalwood incense drifted from an open door that was obscured by hanging strings of cola nut beads. Two men sat on the stoop smoking pipes with incredibly long stems. They wore T-shirts, shorts and sandals and looked like everyone else in the quarter seeking relief from the evening heat. The veins crawling across their corded, rock-hewn forearms, and callused hands bespoke of long weapons training with blades and staves.

The two men watched Bolan approach with supreme disinterest.

When Bolan neared to a few feet, the two men suddenly rose with fluid grace. They flared out heavily developed shoulders and stood in his way like temple guardians carved of stone. Bolan smiled, but the smile he gave them was very sad, as if he were in mourning. He bowed his head toward both men respectfully. *"Asalaam aleikum."*

The two sentries blinked in surprise as Bolan greeted them in Arabic. They bowed back, but their wary eyes were still hooded like hawks considering prey.

"What do you want?" the taller of the two men asked in French.

"I need to speak with Pandekar Soerho." Bolan bowed slightly again. "One of us is fallen."

Bolan took out the knife he had liberated from Pak Widjihartani's corpse in Indonesia. Widjihartani's legion dog tags were wrapped around the hilt. The two men sucked in their breath in dismay. The taller one surveyed Bolan intensely. "And you?"

Bolan pulled up his sleeve. His arm still burned where the tattoo had been scrawled into his skin. The tattoo was not deep, but direct injections of cortisone had been required to get rid of the swelling. The CIA developed inks would dissolve within days. The job had been done by a former Navy SEAL who owned his own tattoo parlor and contracted out tattoos needed by agents going undercover. The man was a pro, and even though the tattoo was less than forty-eight hours old, it looked like Bolan had borne it for years.

The tattoo was of a shield. A dragon was scrawled across its background, and a stylized owl parachuted across the front of it.

The sentries stared at the tattoo and nodded slowly. The taller one took the knife from Bolan and motioned for him to follow them inside.

The scent of sandalwood was very strong. The walls were covered with crossed spears and staves. Short swords and knives with blades that curved in every possible direction were everywhere. Batik prints of gods, heroes and demons covered the patched, steel walls. The incense sticks near the altar had burned low. The evening's instruction was over. Two men swept the floor, and another dusted the altar.

Ali Soerho sat cross-legged on a mat. Bolan scrutinized the *pandekar* carefully as he unfolded his legs and seemed to grow out the mat like a tree. He was a slightly built man who looked to be around fifty. Bolan knew that looks could be quite deceiving in martial-arts masters. Soerho could be anywhere from fifty to seventy, and to have reached the rank of *pandekar* his slight build and gentle features hid his power like silken cloth wrapped around an iron dagger.

The taller of the men escorting Bolan approached the *pandekar* and bowed deeply. He leaned in close to his master and whispered to him for long moments before presenting him with the knife Bolan had brought. Soerho accepted the weapon reverently and went to lay it upon the altar. His man and the two men sweeping fell into rank behind the *pandekar* as he approached Bolan.

The man dusting the altar ceased his cleaning and pulled out a cell phone.

Bolan bowed low to the *pandekar*. The master bowed back and spoke in very rough, halting French. "You speak Arabic?"

Bolan bowed again and replied, "I am only just learning, to further my studies of the Holy Koran."

One of Soerho's men quickly translated. The *pandekar* nodded at Bolan's wisdom. The tall disciple took over as interpreter. "You knew Pak?"

Bolan pulled false foreign legion dog tags up from around his neck. "We served together in the legion. It was there that I converted to Islam."

The man with the phone clicked it shut and went back to his dusting. Bolan noted he was working his way back the way he had just come and was putting himself between Bolan and the door. The *pandekar* spoke through his translator as he gestured at the knife and the dog tags on the altar. "How did you come by these things?"

"How much have you been told?" Bolan countered.

The Javanese had a very rapid discussion in their own language. Bolan decided to interrupt it. "There was an attack. Pak and his men were overcome and killed. We believe it was done by special forces, most likely Australian SAS." Bolan let his eyes harden. "We believe we were betrayed from within."

The taller disciple looked shocked as he translated.

Bolan's face was stony as he openly scrutinized the men before him. One of the disciples flinched as he met the soldier's tombstone stare. The big man had come looking for a traitor. It was very clear that he did not consider them above suspicion. The Executioner repeated himself slowly. "How much have you been told?"

The taller disciple cleared his throat. "Only Ki has been—"

"Where is Ki?" Bolan demanded.

"I am here." A man parted the strings of beads blocking the door. He was short but had almost inhumanly wide shoulders. He was naked save for shorts and sandals. Every muscle in his body stood out in high relief, as did numerous scars, some of which Bolan recognized as bullet and shrapnel wounds. Tattoos crawled along his biceps and shoulders. Both the man's physique and the way he carried himself were reminiscent of a brutal and battle-hardened Bruce Lee. The two men measured each other. Bolan was relieved that the man did not sport the owl and dragon tattoo.

The man wore round, French military dog tags.

Bolan nodded at him. "Ki."

"Ki" looked at the sheathed kris and the dog tags on the altar. He then stared long and hard at Bolan's tattoo. "You served with Pak?"

Bolan threw caution to the wind. "We met in the Pacific. I was in the 5th Foreign Regiment. I spent most of my time at Fantagataufa and a number of the other atolls."

It was a wild gamble. The 5th Foreign Regiment had been stationed in support of France's nuclear testing in the South Pacific. Their activities had great political sensitivity, and the regiment had since been dissolved. Their top-secret duties and subsequent disbandment allowed Bolan to make up almost any kind of story. The Achilles' heel of the ruse was that French-owned atolls were tiny communities. The communities of the legionnaires even tinier. If Ki had served in the same theater, Bolan was toast.

Ki watched Bolan like a hawk as he digested Bolan's story.

Bolan met his gaze without flinching. "How much have you been told?"

Ki never stopped trying to read Bolan's eyes. He looked down at the tattoo on Bolan's arm once more. "I do not know you," he finally announced. "This will require verification."

"Of course." Bolan frowned impatiently but nodded. "I am going to give you a telephone number." He reached slowly into his shirt pocket and pulled out a small pad and a fountain pen. "Memorize it and destroy it."

Bolan flipped open the pad and turned the pen over. Suddenly he pressed the pocket clip.

The pen hissed in Bolan's hand as it shot a stream of pressurized CS tear gas directly into the *pandekar*'s eyes.

Bolan flicked the notebook into Ki's face as the *pandekar* staggered back into his disciples. The blow had no impact but Ki brought his hands up to cover his eyes. Bolan put his thumb on the butt end of the pen and thrust the blunt object into Ki's esophagus.

Ki's knees wobbled as he gagged.

Bolan jumped to put Ki between himself and the rest of the disciples. Blades appeared in their hands.

With his free hand, Bolan ripped the dog tags from around Ki's neck.

The man by the door ripped a rattan stave from the

wall, and it blurred about his body like a propeller as he came for Bolan. The Executioner emptied the rest of the gas-pen at the men surrounding the *pandekar* and broke for freedom as they flinched. Bolan broke sideways and ran at a dead sprint for the eastern wall of the hut. He chose a rusty looking five-foot section of tin siding that had been used to patch a hole in the ancient structure, and hit it like a fullback.

Metal screamed. The rivets holding the siding tore free, and Bolan and the entire section of siding exploded into the night. He rolled in the muck of the alley and came up running.

The disciples boiled out of the hole Bolan had made. They were shouting at the top of their lungs. The soldier could guess what they were yelling to the barrio around them at large.

"Stop him!"

A man rose from a stoop and raised his hands as he stepped into Bolan's path. The Executioner ripped him off his feet with a forearm shiver without breaking stride.

People were coming out of their houses. The big American did not look back, but he could hear a mob swiftly forming behind him. The road ahead began to fill with alarmed citizens. Bolan drew his pistol as he ran, raised the gun in the air and fired off three quick rounds. The flat snap-snap-snapping of the little pistol cut over the sounds of concern and alarm.

The people ahead of Bolan parted like the Red Sea as he ran among them. But the angry mob behind was undeterred.

There was only one avenue of escape, and that was to run.

Bolan retraced his path. It wasn't the quickest way out of the quarter, but it was his safest bet. He knew furious phone calls were crisscrossing, trying to arrange solid resistance ahead to cut him off. Bolan held up his gun to deter anyone who appeared before him. His heart hammered in his chest as he used his size and speed to put distance between himself and the ever increasing mob chasing him.

Bolan caught the scent of cayenne pepper as his lungs heaved. He pushed himself into an all out sprint toward the smell. A pair of dark-skinned men looked up in surprise as he charged past them.

Bolan burst into the Creole quarter. He had no friends here, but neither did the Javanese. He raced across a footbridge and tossed his pistol and holster into the canal below. A gun would not help him here. Behind him, he could hear people shouting at one another in a mix of languages. Creoles began coming out of their houses to see what the ruckus was about.

Many of them carried machetes loosely in their hands.

Bolan ducked down a side alley and quickly lost himself in the maze. He slowed to a walk and let his breathing return to normal. He was still in a dangerous part of town, and he did not expect any Creole to protect him out of Christian charity. But the five thousand Dutch guilders he carried in his belt could buy a great deal of indifference, and probably an anonymous ride back to the embassy, as well.

Bolan held up his prize. The dog tags he had taken from Ki glittered dully in the dim light.

It was time to give Kurtzman something to do.

4

Ki clutched his bruised throat as he spoke hoarsely over the phone. "Pak has been compromised."

The voice on the other end of the line did not sound overly concerned. "How so?"

"They had his dog tags. They followed the trail here. They know he was a legionnaire."

"*Was* a legionnaire," the voice said. "So what?"

Ki's face tightened with more than the pain in the hollow of his throat. "The man took my dog tags and escaped with them."

"Well, now, that is an unfortunate turn of events." The voice paused. "So, just for my edification, this man came in, claiming to be a legionnaire, and then beat up you, the *pandekar*, your friends, stole your dog tags and ran off into the night with them?"

"Yes." Ki's jaws were clenched. "That is about the size of it."

"Tell me, where did he go? I assume you mounted some sort of pursuit?"

"We did. We chased him for some distance through the streets, but he was lightning fast. His attack at the *pandekar*'s was sudden and unorthodox. As was his escape. He is obviously some kind of professional."

"Do you believe he is a legionnaire?" the voice said, this time more in reflection than sarcasm.

Ki had been devoting a great deal of thought to that question. "I do not know. The way he acted, it was clear he is a very experienced soldier. Things like that cannot be faked. Whether he served with Pak in Polynesia…" Ki's scowl returned. "Without a name, that will be very hard to verify, with the unwanted attention it could attract."

"Indeed," the voice agreed. "Tell me, how was his French?"

Ki considered that. "Not perfect, and he spoke with an American accent, but that does not prove anything. The only legionnaires who speak good French are lying Frenchmen."

The voice on the phone snorted derisively. "That is true." The voice lowered. "But in your opinion, is he a legionnaire?"

"He had the dog tags, but I did not get to see them up close. He had the same tattoo as Pak and others who served as security in the atolls." Ki grunted and shook his head. "But my instincts tell me no. I do not believe he is legion."

"That is all I need to hear you say."

Ki rubbed his throat. "So what do we do?"

"Let us assume your instincts are correct, and he is American. To my knowledge, the United States has no military or intelligence assets in Suriname to speak of. The only real place he can take genuine sanctuary or receive any sort of aid is the American Embassy."

Ki spoke bitterly. His hand went to his chest, to the place were a familiar weight was uncomfortably missing. "He has my dog tags."

"Yes, and if he has reached the embassy, he will be able to contact his confederates stateside. It will only be a matter of time before they determine who you are."

"What do you propose we do?"

"Tell the *pandekar* to gather men he trusts. Cover the embassy now, twenty-four hours a day. Sooner or later, he must come out. When he does, you and your men will kill him. I will send Cigarette and Babar to back you up, but you will lead, and you and the *pandekar*'s men must see to finishing the job. If you fail, then whatever kind of stink rises up, it must be a Javanese stink and one that ends in Suriname."

Ki looked at the weapons mounted on the walls. They would be of little use in the coming confrontation. It was the weapons in crates beneath the cellar that would tell the tale now. "And if he somehow escapes us?"

Once more the voice on the other end of the line did not sound concerned. "If he somehow escapes and learns your identity, then he will most certainly come here." The voice paused significantly. "And then I will most certainly kill him."

Secure Communications Room,
U.S. Embassy, Suriname

KURTZMAN WAS CLEARLY unhappy. "Striker, we can't keep plundering French military records."

His brow furrowed on the videophone link. "We're risking a lot. Busting into Suriname's military database would be one thing, but France is a very modern country, with some of the most sophisticated technology in the world. In some areas of technology, France is even ahead of us. And right now, in all honesty, I cannot guarantee you that we're getting in and out undetected. Much less what kind of electronic tracking and countermeasures we may be subjecting ourselves to. If French Military Intelligence catches a whiff of us and goes on a war footing, it's not out of the realm of possibility that they could find us in spite of our fire walls and back doors." Kurtzman shook his head. "I feel the risk may soon be too great."

Bolan considered the problem. "Okay, but what have you got?"

"Well, there are some small hitches with the translation programs. The French foreign legion is kind of archaic in its military terminology. It's also kind of tribal and has a lot of its own slang. Akira's working on it, and—"

"And what have you got, Bear?"

"I've got French Foreign Legion Caporal Ki Gunung. *Caporal* in the Foreign Legion is a lot closer to sergeant in the U.S. or British military as far as authority and responsibilities than what we think of as a corporal."

"What else have you got on him?"

"He's active legion, and didn't change his name when he joined up. He joined the 2nd Parachute Regiment and made it into the Deep Reconnaissance Commandos. The legion's best of the best."

Bolan consulted his map. "The 2nd Parachute Regiment is stationed in Corsica. What's our boy doing in South America?"

"He's a certified hand-to-hand combat and commando instructor." Kurtzman scanned his notes. "It seems he was transferred as a specialist to the 3rd Infantry Regiment and the Jungle Warfare School in French Guiana."

"Interesting," Bolan replied. "But if he's active with the 3rd Infantry Regiment, what is he doing here in Suriname?"

"Well, his current post is less than a hundred miles from where you are now. What he's doing on the wrong side of the Maroni River, we don't know. He could be AWOL, or he could be there with permission. Of course, Suriname and French Guiana do have a disputed border area. He could actually be there on some kind of mission." Kurtzman stared at Bolan fixedly. "That would take a great deal more probing of heavily secured French military files."

"Just do what needs to be done. Hit and git when you feel someone tracking you."

Kurtzman sighed. "Striker, do you have anything to directly tie the French military to terrorist actions taken by al Qaeda?"

Bolan shook his head. "No. All I've got are my instincts, and they're going off like fireworks on the Fourth of July on this one."

"Well that's good enough for me, Striker. You know that."

"Bear, something really nasty is coming down the pipe."

Kurtzman nodded slowly. "So what are you going to do?"

"I'm going to go to French Guiana to poke around."

"YOU'RE NUTS." CIA Station Chief Kira Kiraly gazed at Bolan steadily.

Bolan shrugged. "Yeah, well…"

The station chief blew a lock of hair off her brow. It was just before dawn, and the heat was already rising. "So what are you expecting, again?"

"I'm expecting to get hit, by anywhere from ten to thirty accomplished martial artists and terrorists, armed with anything from machetes and AK-47s up to and exceeding rocket-propelled grenade launchers."

Kiraly nodded once. "Right."

It was clear she believed that Bolan was insane. The station chief was short, blond, sarcastic and very well put together. She didn't look at all like a senior spook.

Bolan knew those were always the best kind.

"Listen." Kiraly shook her head. "I know I've been told to extend you every courtesy, but—"

"What can you do for me?" Bolan smiled winningly. "I'm sorry about it being such short notice."

She held up some keys. "I have a Volvo station wagon."

Bolan shrugged. "Safest car on the road."

"I love that car," the station chief warned. She seemed deadly serious. "The air-conditioning works. You have no idea what kind of premium that is around here."

Kiraly led as they crept around the embassy in the predawn gloom toward the parking area. A pair of Marine embassy guard jeeps and a VW Bug were parked in a line.

Bolan suppressed a grin. Slightly off to one side, parked in the place of honor, gleamed a brown Volvo station wagon with diplomatic plates.

"It's beautiful," Bolan acknowledged.

"Thank you." She searched Bolan for sarcasm. "Maybe it would be best if I drove."

"You don't trust me?"

"I think it would be best if someone drove and someone shot." She looked Bolan up and down with genuine appreciation. "I'm going to trust you on the shooting part."

Bolan shrugged. "I'm thinking the airport is a death trap."

"I agree."

Bolan glanced eastward toward French Guiana. "It's just under two hundred miles to Cayenne."

"Have I shown you the embassy armory?" the station chief inquired. "It's lovely."

THE VOLVO FLEW through the rainforest. After passing Nieuw Amsterdam, the coastal highway had swung inland. They were about thirty miles from the Maroni River and the border with French Guiana. Lush jungle encroached on either side. It was high noon, and the heat was scorching. Sane people in South America spared themselves and their vehicles during this time of day. They passed few cars and saw even fewer people. It was a perfect place for an ambush, and if the enemy was going to do it, they would have to do it soon.

The outside temperature was more than one hundred degrees. It had rained buckets ten minutes earlier, but there was no sign of it save occasional steam rising out of the shelter of the jungle. The Volvo slid down the highway like a blissfully air-conditioned dream at a comfortable sixty-five miles per hour. Comfortable was the word. If Kiraly suddenly floored it, Bolan doubted much more would happen.

The car hit a pothole and the package tied to the luggage rack thumped on the roof, a metallic reminder.

Bolan watched the heat images shimmer on the road ahead. "I know the air-conditioning is on, but why don't you open the windows?"

Kiraly hit the power windows and superheated air swept inside the car interior. The speed of the car did little to mitigate the heat. The sunroof slid open, and the sun blasted down like light through a magnifying glass.

"I see why you love this car," Bolan said.

She shook her head decisively. "You'd better not get this car killed, or…" Her voice trailed off as she caught Bolan's expression. "What?"

The soldier reached for his rucksack on the floor. "Here they come."

In the side mirror Bolan could see a pickup truck pulling out of the heat mirages behind them. It was coming up very fast.

Four motorcycles fanned out around it like outriders of the Apocalypse.

"Drive," Bolan commanded.

Kiraly put the pedal to the floor of her ten-year-old, four-cylinder station wagon. They weren't going to drive their way out of this one.

The pickup was gaining steadily. The motorcycles flew forward like hornets. Each bike carried two men. One man drove; the man behind carried a gun.

They would be in range in seconds.

Bolan clicked down the folding metal foregrip on the Beretta 93-R. The detachable skeleton stock was already affixed. He flicked the machine pistol's selector switch to 3-round-burst mode, grimacing as he turned in his seat. The gunners on the motorcycles were carrying FN-FAL rifles. The big battle rifles were easily capable of chewing a Volvo to pieces. Accuracy would be problematic, but the assassins probably weren't worried about that.

They intended to drive right up and dump their weapons into the car on full-auto at point-blank range.

Bolan stood up through the sunroof, shouldered his weapon and braced himself in the frame. The wind ripped at him as Kiraly pushed the car for all it was worth. Bolan roared over the searing wind, "Keep it straight!"

One of the motorcycles suddenly shot forward like an arrow. The driver's face was lost behind the mirrored visor of his helmet. The gunner's leer of blood lust was openly visible. He struggled to aim his weapon at the rear tires of the Volvo. Bullets ripped divots out of the road surface as his weapon hammered on automatic. The range was too long and the rifle too powerful to control, and his burst climbed away from his target.

The driver gunned his engine and shot forward to close the distance.

Bolan grimaced. Trying to shoot out the tires meant the enemy was going for a capture.

The gunner steadied himself for another burst. Bolan ignored him. He peered along the barrel, then squeezed his trigger.

The driver jerked backward as the burst walked up his chest and neck and punched in the visor of his helmet. The scream of the gunner was lost as the motorcycle went up on its rear wheel and drove out from under the riders. Gunner and driver hit the road in a seventy-five-mile-per-hour pinwheel of breaking bones. The other three motorcycles swerved wildly to avoid the rolling carnage.

Behind them the pickup continued to close in.

Bolan steadied himself and aimed his weapon. The three rifles facing him ripped into life.

The only defense was offense. Bolan stood and shot. A second motorcycle spun out of control as the sol-

dier printed three 9 mm hollowpoints into the driver's
chest. Men and motorcycle rolled in an orgy of twisting metal and rending flesh. The other two gunmen
continued to fire.

Bolan's jaw slammed against the roof of the Volvo,
and he nearly lost his weapon as one of the rear tires
exploded with a lucky hit. He was nearly flung from the
sunroof as Kiraly violently overcorrected to keep the
car on the road. Bolan held on to the luggage rack for
dear life, but the aluminum strut ripped free in his hand.
Only his legs scissored around the headrest kept Bolan
connected to the car as the vehicle fishtailed.

The Executioner squeezed his knees together with
all of his strength as he took the Beretta in both hands.
Kiraly could barely keep the car on the road. Bolan fired
burst after burst trying to compensate for the slewing
vehicle. The motorcycles came on with both rifles blaz-
ing. Bullets chewed into the rear bumper. The remains
of the rear tire shredded away, and the Volvo dipped
sickeningly to one side. Metal screamed as the wheel
bit into the roadway. The roof of the car tore in a line
beside Bolan's elbow, and a whip cracked by Bolan's
ear as a bullet missed his head by inches.

The Beretta recoiled in Bolan's hand and locked
back on empty as he fired off his last burst. The driver
of the closest motorcycle jerked as a bullet took him in
the shoulder, and the gunner behind him rubbernecked
as the second bullet of the burst took him in the face.
The gunner fell off the back motorcycle with his rifle
still firing.

The burst from his dead hand climbed up the back
of his driver.

The motorcycle veered sharply as the driver collapsed and fell into the path of his wingman. Breaking humans and breaking motorcycles bounced and rolled in their death throes across the pavement.

The pickup came on, hitting a body and rolling right over it. Armed men stood in the truck bed clinging to the roll bar. Bolan recognized the shape of an RPG-7 rocket launcher. The truck was closing to within range.

Bolan dropped the Beretta and shoved himself backward to secure his footing in the car. He reached for the flopping remains of the luggage rack and pulled off the bungee cords that held his package.

The Executioner ripped the canvas cover off the M-60 general-purpose machine gun.

He racked the action of the M-60 and pulled open the legs of the bipod. He crouched in the sunroof and leaned into the machine gun's shoulder stock. The lurching of the stricken Volvo made aimed fire almost impossible. Bolan squeezed the trigger and began walking the smoking lines of tracers into the pickup.

The front of the truck sparked with bullet strikes. The Volvo bounced as it hit a bump in the road, and the rest of Bolan's burst went high. There was almost no way to keep the weapon steady. The soldier paused to align his weapon again and fired another burst. The passenger side of the windshield went opaque with bullet strikes before Bolan's burst climbed off aim again.

Flame blossomed around the roof of the truck as the antitank rocket roared out of its launch tube in answer.

Bolan's voice thundered at parade ground decibels. "Right! Right! Right!"

Kiraly yanked the wheel. The football-size warhead of the rocket-propelled grenade flew past the car on a column of black smoke and detonated in the rainforest beyond.

"Brakes!"

Kiraly stood on the brakes, and the car spun screaming into the guardrail. Bolan bounced inside the frame of the sunroof with bone-cracking force. The Volvo careened into a smoking stop. Bolan slammed the M-60 back down across the roof and lined up his sights as the pickup approached.

Bolan squeezed the machine gun's trigger. Tracers walked up the pavement in a line for the front of the truck. The smoking Volvo was finally motionless, and the Executioner had a stable platform from which to use his sights. He leaned into his weapon and held down the trigger. Sparks flew off the grille as he got hits. Sparks flew and bits of metal pinged away from the front. The missile man in the back was desperately ramming a fresh rocket into his launch tube. The hood of the truck flew up as its catch smashed apart. Smoke and flames were whipped by the wind. Bolan paused as the truck closed to one hundred yards, and raised his aim.

The Executioner put his front sight on the driver's side of the windshield and burned the rest of his belt. The popped hood ripped away, and the rest of the windshield collapsed inward. The nose of the dying truck swerved one way and then the other as if someone were wrestling with the wheel, and then spun as if someone had violently won the fight.

The truck veered across the road, hit the guardrail and somersaulted off the highway. The men in the back went flying.

Bolan's spare belt of ammo for the M-60 had miraculously stayed attached to the canvas tied to the roof. He laid the belt into the feed ramp and clacked it shut. "Go, get us away from the scene and then pull off the road, we'll—"

"We've got problems," Kiraly said.

Bolan glanced around. It was only a two-lane highway. A few hundred yards ahead a pair of military-style jeeps blocked the road in a V formation. There was nowhere to run, and the Volvo was in no shape for a chase, anyway. Bolan racked the M-60's action. "Floor it."

Metal screamed as the remaining rear tire clawed for traction and the side panels sparked themselves free of the guardrail. A man stood beside each jeep carefully aiming a rifle across the hood. Bolan slid back down into the car.

"Close your eyes," he said.

Kiraly flinched at the deafening blast as Bolan shot out the windshield. He pulled up his knee and kicked out the sagging glass panel and then shoved the M-60 forward onto the hood.

The Volvo limped up to forty miles per hour. Kiraly shook her head in horror at the apocalyptic game of chicken. The riflemen ahead began firing.

"Don't stop," Bolan said as he began triggering bursts from first at one jeep and then the other. The bipod slid on the hood, and Bolan's shots were all over the map. Aimed fire began hitting the front of the Volvo. Bullets tore into the grille. Bolan's side mirror was shot away, and Kiraly flinched and screamed as a bit of the headrest by her ear disappeared. Steam spewed from bullet holes in the hood. Kiraly kept her foot on the gas, and the dying Volvo lurched on like a Swedish kamikaze.

Bolan fired burst after burst and suddenly the two jeeps were right in front of them. The two riflemen hurled themselves away from the impending carnage. Bolan yanked the red-hot machine gun back into the car and clasped it across his chest.

The Volvo hit the roadblock at forty-seven miles per hour.

The jeeps spun away in opposite directions as the front of the Volvo folded like an accordion. Front and side air bags blew forth from the safety panels and violently expanded to obscure Bolan's world as the Volvo sailed on. The car burst through the guardrail and came to a halt against a forty-foot ironwood tree.

Bolan ignored the stars in his vision and the coppery taste of blood in his mouth. He ripped free the knife on his belt and gutted the air bags pressing against him. He yanked the door handle but nothing happened as the air bags deflated around him. The soldier threw his shoulder once, twice and the third time his door burst open. He fell to the mud and gravel, clutching the M-60. He lurched up and slammed the weapon across the roof of the vehicle.

A gunshot rang out instantly, and something plucked at the collar of Bolan's shirt.

He clamped down his trigger and sprayed an arc of bullets before him. He caught sight of the two riflemen crouched beside one of the mangled jeeps. The Executioner kept his trigger down and forced them under cover with sheer firepower.

Kiraly's .45-caliber Glock pistol began barking on rapid semiauto from the driver's-side window. Bolan maintained fire and riddled the jeep into smoking ruin. He let off the trigger and glared down his sights. Brass shell casings rolled across the pavement. There were no other sounds except the ticking, hissing, dripping and steaming sounds of dead and dying automobiles.

The soldier kept his hand on the trigger as he slid the M-60's sling over his shoulder. He crouched and came around the Volvo with the machine gun in the hip-assault position. He looked both ways, but nothing moved. Save for the jungle itself, there was no cover to be had except for the destroyed automobiles. Bolan crossed the road covering the jeep. He stepped around and found what he had been expecting.

Broken glass, spent shell casings and blood.

The Executioner walked to the edge of the highway and swung a leg over the guardrail. There was a bloody handprint on the curved metal. Bolan took a deep breath and scanned ahead. Six feet away the jungle was a solid wall. He looked down into the mud beside the highway. There were boot prints.

Two sets of them.

They were clearly two different sizes, but both sets of prints had the exact same pattern of tread marks. The smaller set of prints faltered and smeared twice on the right hand side. The larger set grew deeper. Bolan nodded. One of the men was definitely wounded. He memorized the pattern of the treads for a future sketch and walked back to the road. He picked up a couple of his opponent's spent shell casings and pocketed them and then returned to the car.

Kiraly lay back like a wet rag in the driver's seat. Her nose was broken and so was her left hand. Her spent Glock lay in her lap with the action racked back on an empty chamber. She gave Bolan a bruised smile and reached up to pat the cracked dashboard.

"Volvo. Safest car on the road today."

5

Hotel Cayenne, French Guiana

"What do you think?"

Kurtzman responded over the videophone link. "Nice piece of work there."

Bolan glanced at the sketch he had made of the tread patterns he had seen in the mud by the highway. "So what did you make of them?"

The computer expert hit a key and an image popped up on Bolan's screen. It was a pair of combat boots. They were distinctive in that they had a leather flap and two buckles in addition to the laces. "They're standard French military issue, and, not surprisingly, standard issue to the French Foreign Legion, as well." Kurtzman grinned. "Like I said, nice piece of detective work there."

"What did the Cowboy make of the shell casings?"

"French manufactured .223 ammunition." Kurtzman punched another key, and John Kissinger's report popped up on the screen. "Cowboy says whoever those two boys shooting at you in Suriname might be, they were firing the latest generation FAMAS G-2 rifle, and doing it with French army ammo."

Bolan grimaced as he forced himself to stretch. The bouncing around he'd taken in the Volvo during the battle and the subsequent crash left his body feeling like he'd lost a bar fight.

He considered the battle. "The guys on the motorcycles and the truck were more of the *pandekar*'s boys. Had to be. I'm betting the rocketeer was our friend Ki. The two guys at the roadblock were our real players."

Kurtzman raised an eyebrow. "Legionnaires?"

"Actually, I'm thinking French Foreign Legion deep reconnaissance commandos." Bolan shrugged and rolled his neck to work out the kinks. "But I can't prove that yet.

"The guys on the motorcycles were fearless, but they were strictly local talent. The other two were highly trained professionals. They engaged with aimed fire and took out the vehicle. Our boys closed in for the kill, and when I opened up and wounded one of them they extracted under fire, right into open jungle. If I had to bet, I'd say those two guys went 'escape and evade' and walked home all fifty miles through the rainforest. They were ghosts."

Kurtzman was clearly troubled. "Deep reconnaissance commando kind of ghosts."

"That's my current theory." Bolan shrugged. "Until I can come up with something better. You get me my stuff?"

Kurtzman nodded. "You have a full war load in position in a storage facility near the edge of town. As for calling on any local assistance or assets, it keeps getting thinner. At least Suriname had an embassy. French Guiana is, literally, still a French owned colony. The U.S. has almost no presence. What little we have are more interested in snooping around the satellite launch facility at Kourou. Their main function probably has more to do with bribing French engineers for rocket technology than engaging in any kind of special operations, but they've been told to offer you every professional courtesy should you come knocking."

Bolan nodded. Kira Kiraly was doing what she could to drum up support with her contacts. "I'll keep it in mind," he said.

"One other thing." Kurtzman flashed a guilty smile. "Akira did some snooping…strictly against my orders, of course."

Bolan nodded.

"Your friend Ki was on *permissionaire* in Suriname."

"*Permissionaire?*"

"Official vacation leave. Normally legionnaires aren't allowed to leave France when on vacation, or French territory if they're serving abroad, so those stationed in French Guiana have to stay in-country, but they do make official exceptions according to circumstances. Ki is a hand-to-hand combat instructor at the Jungle Warfare school. He was on leave in Suriname at least partly to officially sharpen up his skills at the *pandekar*'s school."

Bolan frowned. That threw a minor monkey wrench into his theories about a Foreign Legion plot. It made it look much more like Kurtzman had first postulated. That the opponents he'd encountered were simply Javanese renegades, who had met in French service and were acting on their own. Bolan wished he'd had time to check out the crashed pickup, but he and Kiraly had been forced to get away from the battle zone as quickly as possible.

Kurtzman read his mind. "I wonder if Ki is still alive?"

"You know, that's a good question." Bolan rose. He was still battered and bruised, but rest would have to wait. "Let's go find out."

French Foreign Legion Jungle Warfare School

THE DUCATI S4 Fogarty motorcycle skidded to a halt in a spray of gravel. The Executioner rocked the bike back on its stand and dismounted in front of the guardhouse. He pulled off his helmet while the legionnaire in the booth gaped in awe at the gleaming Italian motorcycle. Bolan grinned like an idiot as he approached the gate. He noted the legionnaire's rifle lay propped in a corner. The legionnaire did, however, have a Beretta 92-G service pistol holstered at his hip. He wore his white kepi hat and massive red ceremonial epaulets on his shoulders for guard duty with uniform shorts in deference to the tropical heat. He picked up his clipboard and walked out to meet Bolan.

"Hi!" Bolan waved in a friendly fashion. "I mean...*bonjour!*"

The legionnaire looked Bolan up and down. He rolled his eyes in infinite disgust as he sized him up. Clearly he thought Bolan was an idiot. The legionnaire replied in English, with a thick Irish accent.

"This is the Jungle Warfare School. If you wish to join the French Foreign Legion, you must go to an official French Foreign Legion recruitment center." The legionnaire raised a weary eyebrow at Bolan. "They are all located in France. I can give you a list of the recruitment centers if you wish."

Bolan's smile turned up in wattage. "What makes you think I'd want to join this crazy outfit?"

The legionnaire's jaw dropped for a split second and then set in a hard line. He drew himself to his full height as he lowered his clipboard and his right hand drifted toward the butt of his pistol. "State your business."

"Hey, speaking of crazy, you seen Ki Gunung, around?"

"He is on leave." The legionnaire's cheeks colored. "State your business."

Bolan smiled happily. He doubted whether the guardsman was going to ask him again. "Give him a message for me, would you?"

The guard brought his clipboard back up with robot-like formality. "State your message. I will see that he receives it."

"Tell him…" Bolan made a show of searching for the right words. The legionnaire slowly lowered his clipboard.

Bolan held up his hand. Ki's dog tags dangled from between his fingers. "Tell him if he wants these back he's going to have to come and get them. I'm not hard to find."

"Hey!" The legionnaire blinked in alarm and his hand went to his pistol. "You—"

The Executioner closed his hand around the dog tags and pistoned his fist into the point of the guard's chin. The legionnaire's head snapped back. His eyes rolled back in his head, and his knees buckled and folded. Bolan was already back on his bike as the guard slumped against his booth and slid unconscious to the ground. The soldier revved the Ducati's massive twin-cylinder engine and sprayed the fallen guard and the guardhouse with gravel for good measure. He shot out onto the road like an arrow shot from a bow.

If Ki was still alive, the Executioner suspected his leave had just been cut short.

Hotel Cayenne

SOMEONE WAS in the room.

Bolan could smell cigarette smoke. He put his key in the lock and pushed the door open with the toe of his shoe. Two men were slouching in the chairs by the window smoking.

Bolan entered the room and threw his bag down on the bed. *"Bonjour."*

The taller, lankier one smiled and blew a smoke ring. *"Bonjour."*

The man had a Gallic nose and jaw like a shovel. His partner was blond and movie-star handsome. Both men had deep suntans and wore tropical-weight suits of decent cut. To Bolan they looked like agents from a Eurotrash episode of *Miami Vice*. He swiftly sized them up. These men were not legionnaires. If they were, they would have attacked Bolan as he came through the door and pounded him into oblivion. Nor did they have the aggressive posture of police dealing with a possible suspect. They were lounging around his hotel room like they owned it, and looking at Bolan like cats examining a mouse with nowhere to run.

They were French Intelligence.

"Well, *mon ami*." The bigger man scratched his stubble and spoke English with a Southern France accent.

"Tell me, just who are you?"

"You've already checked my visa and my entry records. You know exactly who I am," the Executioner replied.

"Well, of course we do." The big man shrugged in a supremely French manner. "But…who are you, exactly?"

One look told Bolan these were the kind of men who made people disappear.

The blonde pulled something from under his coat and set it on the little table by the window. The M-26 Advanced Taser was capable of pumping ten thousand watts into anyone who found themselves on the wrong end of it. The weapon rested inches from the blonde's hand. The twin probes and laser sight were aimed at Bolan. Blondie's smile was painted on his face.

The big man rose from his chair and reached under his coat. Bolan suspected it wasn't a stun gun that was about to make an appearance.

Bolan rammed his heel into the man's solar plexus and stomped him back down into his chair. A revolver fell from his hand and clattered to the floor. The French agent's arms and legs sucked in like an agonized spider. Bolan booted him under the jaw to put him out of the fight.

The ruby beam of the Taser's laser sight drew a brilliant dot on Bolan's chest as he turned. The Taser's compressed air cartridge chuffed and the probe flew forth trailing its wire and hit Bolan square over the heart. Blondie snarled in triumph. The Taser's power pack crackled as he held down the trigger.

Blondie's triumph died on his face as Bolan turned on him. The Frenchman took the Taser in both hands and fired a second probe. The range was point-blank. Bolan took the hit in the stomach.

The concealable soft body armor the Executioner wore under his shirt was Threat Level I and rated to stop a 9 mm round. The air-compressed probe stood no chance, and the woven Kevlar and nylon of Bolan's armor was a nearly perfect electrical insulator.

Blondie held the Taser before him still uselessly pumping the power. He tried to rise even as his left hand whipped around behind his back. Bolan shot his hand forward and wrapped it around Blondie's neck. He clamped down to cut off the carotid arteries and yanked the Frenchman forward.

Bolan head-butted him directly between the eyes.

The agent fell unconscious into his chair. Bolan swiftly patted down the two Frenchmen. Their ID cards identified them as Roland Aretos and Alain Reno, respectively. Both men were heavily armed. The French had come to play, and they were prepared to play rough. Bolan shook his head as his suspicions were confirmed.

He had attracted the attention of Action Direct. How exactly he had done that by beating up the day guard at the gate of the Jungle Warfare School was an interesting question.

The math was pretty simple. There was only one way Action Direct could have gotten onto him this quickly. They already had an operation in motion, and he had walked into it unannounced. The soldier was grim as he left his hotel.

The stakes had just gotten higher.

6

Bolan sat at a café table. It was early evening, and most of French Guiana had left work.

The sun was setting behind the hills in the west, and the view of the ocean was gorgeous in the dying rays of the sun. He wondered when French Intelligence would make its next contact. It had been twenty-four hours, and though he had switched hotels, he had deliberately driven the gleaming Ducati at brazen speeds through the capital and parked it openly on the streets where he'd stopped in his travels. The bike was parked a few yards away.

He checked his watch and decided to order some food. He was exhausted and needed to maintain his energy. Bolan's hand froze as he raised it toward the waiter. The howl of a turbo-charged engine on the street told him the meal would have to wait.

A racing-green convertible screeched to a halt beside his bike. Every head in the café turned. The Executioner gazed in open appreciation at the person who stepped out of the car.

She was one of the most drop-dead gorgeous women he had ever seen.

The woman's black hair was cut short and fell around her head like a dark, tousled helmet. She wore a white cotton sundress. The rays of the sun striking her from behind silhouetted her legs through the fabric. She strode directly to Bolan's table, took a chair and poured herself into it. Bolan glanced at her, smiling.

Frenchwomen knew something about making an entrance.

The woman draped herself over the back of the chair and stared at Bolan intently. Her olive complexion was set off magnificently by a startling pair of eyes. One was blue and the other green. She continued to stare at Bolan without blinking.

She extended her hand. "My name is Jolie Erulin."

Bolan took her hand in his and gave it a friendly squeeze. "Matt Cooper, and I am very pleased to make your acquaintance." Bolan motioned the waiter over. "Whatever the lady wishes.

"Whiskey." The woman's dual-colored gaze did not break contact. "You beat the shit out of Roland and Alain," she said.

Bolan nodded.

"You beat the shit out of Legionnaire Doherty at the Jungle Warfare School, and he was only doing his duty."

Bolan felt a little bad about that but not enough to lose any sleep. "Well…yeah."

The waiter brought the woman her whiskey. She took a hefty swallow and savored it a moment. "You think you can just waltz into the territorial possessions of France and beat the shit out of our legionnaires without fear of reprisal?"

Bolan considered his response. "What if I told you I was acting in reprisal?"

Her lips pursed a moment. "I would ask you to clarify that statement."

"What if I told you that a French legionnaire tried to kill me in Suriname. I sought him out at the school, and left him a message. Admittedly at Legionnaire Doherty's expense."

"You are speaking of Ki Gunung, a highly decorated soldier of the legion. However, this might explain why the CIA agent Kira Kiraly came across the border with you and required medical attention here in Cayenne."

Bolan smiled. "You mean Cultural Attaché Kiraly."

"Whatever." The Frenchwoman rolled her eyes. "Cultural Attaché" was synonymous with "CIA spook" in every nation on earth. "So, tell me, why do you feel the need to engage in feuds with legionnaires on leave in Suriname?"

Bolan locked his gaze with the French agent's and held it implacably. "Because I killed his friend on the island of Champaka Putih."

The beautiful face froze, and Bolan knew he'd hit pay dirt. Action Direct had an ongoing mission in French Guiana, and they were watching the French Foreign Legion.

Just like he was.

Jolie Erulin regained her poker face. "You are a very intriguing man, and I am enjoying our conversation very much."

"Thank you. I couldn't imagine a lovelier companion to enjoy the sunset with."

"Yes, thank you. But you must forgive me if I take my leave and speak with my superiors before we exchange any more information."

They'd exchanged exactly nothing. Bolan had done all the talking. "Not at all. I am at your convenience."

Erulin's eyes narrowed slightly. "I must ask you, out of professional courtesy, not to engage in any more acts of reprisal for the next twenty-four hours, or until we speak further."

"I'll be here tomorrow at this same time." Bolan set down his glass. "But I'm not sure if I can promise you anything beyond that."

"I thought not." Erulin finished her whiskey and regarded Bolan carefully. "I am afraid our conversation has been somewhat one sided. Allow me to share with you, then, some information you may find most useful here in French Guiana."

"What's that?"

The French agent leaned in close and dropped her voice low. "Legionnaires who have applied for and been granted a leave slip by their commanding officer are allowed to be absent from camp between the hours of 1730 to 0530. You are a hunted man."

7

"Who is this man?"

Cigarette avoided the gaze of the Commander. Babar met it with difficulty.

The Commander shook his head slowly. "That is information I would dearly like to acquire."

"Yes." Babar let out a long breath. "And since we speak of information, is it true that Action Direct is now involved?"

"Yes, Babar. It is true," the Commander confirmed.

Babar looked profoundly disturbed at the news. Action Direct operators abroad had a reputation for killing people perceived as enemies of France and asking questions later.

Cigarette voiced Babar's concern. "So, what do we do? The situation is leaving our control."

"The situation is under our complete control," the Commander countered. "We always knew sooner or later we would have to deal with Action Direct. This stranger's appearance has worked in our favor, and forced them to show their hand early." The Commander smiled. "And make no mistake, the plan would not have gone forward from the very beginning without my having a line on Action Direct."

Babar and Cigarette smiled in relief. It never paid to underestimate the Commander. If he said he had a card to play with Action Direct, they did not doubt him for a second.

The Commander revealed more of his teeth. "This American's brawl at the Jungle Warfare School also serves our purpose. Every legionnaire in French Guiana has applied for leave to be out of camp tonight." The Commander leaned back in his chair and lit a cigar. "The officers are quite upset about the situation at the gate. As I understand it, they are being quite lenient with their leave books. Starting at 1730 hours tonight, the American is a hunted man."

The Commander took a long pull on his cigar, amused. "Furthermore, someone, I know not who…"

Babar and Cigarette laughed.

"Has sent anonymous letters to our local newspapers," the Commander continued. "These letters state that this man is a deserter and a traitor to the legion, and the legion will appreciate any and all help from the citizens of France. A small reward is mentioned along with the patriotic duty of all Frenchmen." The Commander's smile was beatific. "I do not think the officers, given their current mood, will do anything to contradict these letters."

Babar smiled to reveal a mouthful of gold teeth. His voice dropped a happy, dangerous octave. "So there is no place he can hide."

"Oh, my friend, hiding is all that he can do. He has no safe haven in French Guiana. Everywhere he must hide or skulk in the shadows. His ability to operate has been severely compromised." The Commander leaned forward and fixed Babar with his stare. "Now, what can you tell me about him?"

"He was big." Babar shook his head in memory. "Not as big as me—"

"Who is?" the Commander said.

"And fast." Cigarette held up his wounded arm. "He came out of the smashed car like a jumping jack with a heavy machine gun. Shooting everywhere at once. Babar and I are lucky to be alive."

Babar nodded in unhappy agreement. "Yes, Cigarette is correct. This man, he had skills. As good or better as any man among us."

"Yes. An operator." The Commander puffed on his cigar reflectively. "A real American cowboy."

Cigarette shrugged. "So what do we do?"

The Commander shook his head absently. "Nothing."

"Nothing?" Both Babar and Cigarette sat up in their chairs.

"Nothing," the Commander repeated. "Because that is exactly what this American has. Nothing. And I do not propose to give him anything further. All he has is a cold dead trail. It started in Indonesia, he followed it to Suriname, and it has ended here in French Guiana. He has nothing to go on. And whatever theories he may have, not in his worst nightmares does he even begin to suspect what is to come. What can he do? He has antagonized the legion, Action Direct and the civilian population. He can cower in the shadows and do nothing, or he can show his face in the streets and have it smashed in." He leaned forward and made a meaningful fist. "Just one week is all he has, and after that, he is superfluous. All he will be able to do is weep."

Cigarette and Babar nodded as they contemplated what was to come. Cigarette lit up a Galois and took a nervous drag. "Still, I do not like doing nothing."

The Commander smiled again. "I said we would do nothing. I did not say nothing would happen to the American in the meantime." He took a languorous puff on his cigar. "Even though he has nothing, there is still a loose end he has not tied up, and I believe we all know someone who owes something very special to our American friend. Death surrounds him."

Cigarette and Babar smiled. The American had failed in that regard.

The Commander lounged back in his chair. "Where can he go?"

French Foreign Legion Jungle Warfare School

THE GUARDS GAPED at Bolan.

Getting out of Cayenne hadn't been easy. The situation had quickly become untenable. Between the hours of 1730 to 0530 he was a hunted man, and more and more legionnaires were appearing on the streets at all hours. The Executioner had made his way down to the motorcycle shop, bought the only other Ducati S4 in French Guiana and got the hell out of Dodge.

The legionnaires at the gate of the Jungle Warfare School were shocked. Their hands went to their pistols.

"I would like to speak with someone in command," Bolan told them.

The two guards looked at each other and spoke rapidly in a language that was not French.

Bolan tried again. "It is important that I speak with your commanding officer. If you call him and tell him who is at the gate, I believe he will wish to see me at once."

One guard drew his pistol and held it on Bolan with both hands. The other man retreated to the guard shack without taking his eyes off Bolan and began speaking rapid French into the telephone. He hung up, drew his pistol and pointed it at Bolan. "You will remain here."

The soldier nodded and waited patiently.

It took no time at all for a squad of legionnaires to come pounding up to the gate. Every man among them carried an assault rifle with the bayonet fixed. Bolan kept his face pleasant as Legionnaire Doherty stepped forward. The legionnaire was struggling valiantly to keep his emotions under control. "You will accompany me to the commandant's office." His teeth ground as he gestured at the men surrounding Bolan. "These men are for your protection. I must ask you to surrender any weapons you may be carrying."

Bolan raised both of his arms out to the sides. "I am unarmed."

Two legionnaires swiftly patted Bolan down and then nodded the all-clear to Doherty. The soldiers formed a block around Bolan as Doherty shouted out orders. They trotted down the short one-lane road to the camp. Legionnaires looked up from their duties about camp and began shouting and pointing at Bolan. The words came in a dozen different languages, and none of them sounded friendly. However, nothing more hostile than words came his way. Bolan was betting on the absolute adherence of the legion to professionalism, duty and discipline.

No one in the camp would attack him without express orders from the officers.

What the officers would do might be a different story.

The French Foreign Legion also had a reputation for brutality and vindictiveness.

Bolan and his honor guard crossed the camp and came to a small building. The guard detail turned and fanned out before the increasing mob of angry legionnaires forming around them. Doherty motioned for Bolan to follow him inside. They quickly marched down a hallway and came to the door at the end. Doherty gave two swift knocks. A voice from within beckoned.

Doherty opened the door. A thin man looking to be in his forties sat behind the desk of a Spartan office. Doherty closed the door behind them and snapped to attention and saluted.

Doherty finished his salute by slapping his leg and took his position by the door.

Bolan and the commandant measured each other. The nameplate on the desk read Commandant Michel Marmion.

"Please, sit. Be at ease. I will speak in English for your benefit." The commandant gestured at the chair facing his desk. "Cigarette?"

"No, thank you. And thank you for seeing me on such short notice."

"Oh, well, it was that or let you be torn to pieces, and, to be honest, you intrigue me." The commandant lit a cigarette and gazed at Bolan speculatively. "Tell me, do you really wish to pick a fight with the entire Jungle Warfare School?"

"No, I only wished to attract the attention of a single member of it. The incident at the gate was regrettable."

Doherty glowered.

The commandant's gaze grew troubled. "You speak of Caporal-Chef Ki Gunung."

"Yes."

"Why is it you wish to fight him?" Marmion leaned forward. "Is this some sort of personal vendetta? If it is, I am afraid that as his commanding officer I cannot allow him to participate. Further, should you insist on your attempts to force a confrontation, I must warn you I will do everything in my power, which is not inconsiderable, to make your stay in French Guiana as short and unpleasant as possible."

"I understand completely." Bolan gauged the officer before him, and decided he stood a better chance with the iron honor of the legion than he would playing games with Action Direct. "But I believe that Caporal-Chef Gunung is a traitor to the legion."

Bolan heard Doherty's knuckles pop as he curled his hands into fists. He ignored the legionnaire and kept his gaze on the commandant.

Marmion stared at Bolan for long moments. "I am going to allow you the opportunity to explain that statement."

"There was an operation in Indonesia—"

"By and for whom?" the commandant interrupted.

"There was an operation in Indonesia—some Dutch missionaries had been kidnapped. Perhaps you were aware of it?"

"Vaguely. It was in the news. It was some sort of terrorist act. I believe al Qaeda was suspected," Marmion acknowledged. "I understand the missionaries were successfully rescued."

"Yes, during that operation it was discovered that a former legionnaire named Pak Widjihartani was intimately involved. He was Indonesian and had served the Foreign Legion in the 5th Pacific Regiment.

Intelligence led the investigation to Suriname, where—"

"Where Caporal-Chef Gunung was on leave." The commandant leaned back in his chair. "Gunung is a suspect?"

"More than that. Investigation found direct evidence linking Gunung and his associates in Suriname to the terrorists in Indonesia. Gunung served with Pak in the 5th Pacific Regiment. I believe he is part of a plot, with at least nominal ties to al Qaeda." Bolan locked his gaze with the commandant. "I do not believe he is working alone."

Marmion's face was tight as he turned to Doherty. "Fetch Ilyanov."

Doherty saluted and bolted from the office. Bolan heard a door open down the hallway, and two sets of boots tramped back to the commandant's office. A large, blue-eyed, blond man accompanied Doherty. He saluted the commandant sharply, but his blue eyes were cold and never left Bolan.

Marmion gestured at the man towering in the doorway. "This is Sergeant-Chef Vasily Ilyanov. Ilyanov, this is…" Marmion shrugged. "This is a man who says that Caporal-Chef Gunung is working for terrorists and is a traitor to the legion."

Ilyanov's blue eyes went arctic.

Bolan smiled. "You're Gestapo?"

Ilyanov smiled, but it did not reach his eyes. "Gestapo" was a legion nickname for their own internal security.

Marmion nodded. "Sergeant-Chef Ilyanov is head of security here in the camp, among his other duties. He also has the advantage of having served in the 5th Regiment in the Pacific. Ilyanov, did you ever serve with a Legionnaire Pak Widjihartani?"

Ilyanov thought a moment. "Yes, he was on the Fantagataufa atoll at the same time I was, and served in the same security detail as I did."

"What about Gunung?"

"He was not on Fantagataufa, but I had seen him in the islands on leave. French Tahiti is a small place, and there are only so many places legionnaires on leave can go."

"This man says that Widjihartani was involved in terrorist activities in Indonesia, and that Gunung was in contact with him, and participating, in one way or another. To your knowledge, did they fraternize during their service in the Pacific?"

"I could not swear to it." Ilyanov looked unhappily from the commandant to Bolan. "But I believe yes. However that is not unusual. They were both Indonesian. In the legion, Germans tend to fraternize with Germans, Asians with Asians." Ilyanov shrugged. "Russians with Russians, and—"

"Muslims with Muslims," Bolan said.

"Well, yes," the Russian admitted. "They do tend to congregate and take prayers together. In a legion of strangers, one seeks out one's own."

"Ilyanov." Marmion's jaw set. "How many Muslim legionnaires have we here in the camp?"

"Few." The big Russian scratched his chin as he did a mental head count. "Caporal Atrache is Algerian. Caporal-Chef Sahin is a Turk."

"Any others?"

"Not to my knowledge, Commandant, but I will look into it."

"Good. Put Sahin and Atrache under observation, but be subtle about it. Look into the record of their leaves during service. Gunung was allowed special permission to visit Suriname. I want to see if they have had any similar excursions. I also want you to examine Sahin's and Atrache's initial enlistment and reenlistment interviews. Look for any discrepancies or anything that might seem relevant to the current circumstances. Report what you find directly to me. Is that understood?"

Ilyanov snapped to attention. "By your order, Commandant."

Marmion turned and gave Bolan a hard look. "Now, you must give me a reason to confide in you, much less prevent Ilyanov and Doherty from dragging you outside and ripping you a new rectum to the cheers of my men."

There was absolutely no reason for Marmion to confide in Bolan. He could not tell Marmion who he was. He had assaulted the guard at the gate and then come into Marmion's office and dropped a bomb in his lap. A bomb that would be very hard to prove or disprove. Bolan glanced around the office and his eyes fell on a framed photograph on the wall. A much younger looking Michel Marmion with lieutenant's bars on his uniform wore a green beret, and stood in front of a French AMX-10 wheeled reconnaissance vehicle. A black man in U.S. desert camouflage and mirrored sunglasses also wearing lieutenant's bars stood beside him. They had their arms around each other's shoulders. Both men were holding up glasses of wine and smiling as they toasted the camera. The desert stretched out behind them.

The American was wearing a black beret.

"You were in Desert Storm," Bolan said.

Marmion nodded. "We call it Operation Dagger in France, but yes."

Bolan pointed at the picture. "Assuming that man is still alive, what if he called you within the next twenty-four hours and told you I was good people?"

Marmion snorted. "I believe my friend retired some years ago. It has been many years since we have been in touch. However, were he to call me, tomorrow, and personally inform me that the man who assaulted my camp is to be trusted with matters of legion, if not French national security itself, that would indeed give me pause."

"Give me his name and his unit, and I'll have him contact you personally within twenty-four hours," the Executioner said.

"Very well." Marmion took a pen from his pocket and quickly scrawled a few lines. "I cannot promise you anything."

"I understand that." Bolan's smile was sincere. "Given the circumstances, you have been more than understanding."

"Of course I must contact my superiors. French Military Intelligence will undoubtedly become involved."

Bolan played his second card. "Action Direct already is."

Marmion's face fell. "Really."

Bolan knew his card was a winner. The world was the same all over. The CIA and the FBI in the U.S., the SVR and the GRU in Russia, and Action Direct and French Military Intelligence, it made no difference where you went. Civil and military intelligence services were always at odds with one another, if not downright at war.

The commandant's fingers drummed the desktop. "You have been contacted by Action Direct?"

"My initial welcome by the legion was warmer."

"I see." Marmion scowled. "Doherty has informed me that he received a phone call saying what café you could be located at the other day, but he arrived too late. These were the actions of Action Direct?"

"I am almost sure of it," Bolan stated. "I was contacted by a woman claiming the name Jolie Erulin."

"Ilyanov, check on that." Marmion gave Bolan a thin smile. "I will wait twenty-four hours before I make my decision on whether or not to let Ilyanov and Doherty cripple you."

Bolan glanced at the two legionnaires. "I appreciate that."

Marmion sighed heavily. "Ilyanov, what is Caporal-Chef Gunung's current status?"

The big Russian checked his watch. "Caporal-Chef Gunung's leave ended over seventy-two hours ago. He remains absent without leave."

Bolan glanced at the Russian. It seemed both Action Direct and the legion were aware something was up with Gunung.

The soldier turned to Marmion. "As I mentioned, Gunung was encountered in Suriname. There is a chance he was severely injured or killed."

Marmion accepted this without comment.

The coldness returned to Ilyanov's eyes. "Permission to speak freely, Commandant."

"Granted."

Ilyanov looked at Bolan. "It would be best for you if he is dead. If he is not, he is hunting you, and he is a very dangerous man. If he is alive, and what you say is true, it shall be my job to hunt him down." The big Russian leaned in close and thrust out his jaw. "And if he is alive, and what you say turns out to be lies, then we shall hunt you together."

8

Roura, French Guiana

"So how did it go?"

The laptop and the portable satellite link showed Kurtzman sharp and clear on the screen. It was the best intelligence suite Bolan could manage on the back of a motorcycle. He had driven south twelve miles to the town of Kourou and rented a bungalow by the river. Even with the commandant's calling off the dogs, the capital was still teeming with patriotic citizens of France who wanted to beat the living hell out of him. Out in the sticks, he could still pass for a tourist.

"Commandant Marmion wasn't happy. He already knew that Gunung was AWOL, and nothing I told cheered him up. Speaking of the commandant, I need you to locate a former U.S. Army Ranger captain, Royce Cunningham, 2nd Battalion. He knew Marmion during Desert Storm. He just might be the key to getting me some legion cooperation."

"I'm on it. What about this Russian, Ilyanov?" Kurtzman asked.

"Well, he's Gestapo, legion internal security. He's big, and he is angry."

"What do you think that means to you, Striker?"

Bolan considered the big Russian. "The legion has a reputation for taking care of its own. At one time they were known for tracking down deserters and killing them. If he gets convinced I'm right, I wouldn't want to be Gunung."

"I gather he doesn't like you much, either."

"I don't see him trying to kill me in cold blood, at least not without some kind of sanction, official or otherwise." Bolan thought about the hard glints in Ilyanov's and Doherty's eyes. "But given the chance, I think there's nothing he'd love more than to gather up some of the boys and send me home on a gurney."

"So that still leaves Gunung as your main concern."

Bolan nodded. "If he's still alive."

"Yeah, and if he is, he won't stop at sending you home in traction. He's more likely to use some messed up Indonesian cutlery and send you home in a bag, in chunks, and I doubt he'll be alone."

"Speaking of his buddies, I also got a line on two legionnaires in the camp. A Turk named Sahin and an Algerian named Atrache."

"I'll try to track them down." Kurtzman punched a few keys. "And that dovetails in nicely with your two shooters wearing French combat boots at the roadblock."

"It would, except that one of the shooters was wounded, and by his tracks it was bad enough that he had to lean on his friend. A legionnaire limping with a bullet wound wouldn't be able to keep it a secret very long. It's a small camp, and those guys run ten miles every morning before they get their coffee and croissants. That is, if they're not humping their rucksacks through the rain forest on training missions. They also assemble at parade about seventeen times a day. Neither Marmion or Ilyanov acted like either one was missing or mysteriously wounded. I got the impression that Sahin and Atrache were in camp. I also got the impression that no one else was AWOL other than Gunung."

Kurtzman spoke again. "You think we have two more legionnaires in this little cabal, and they are out on leave."

"That's what I'm thinking."

Kurtzman scowled. "So you have two, possibly three commandos gunning for you, along with as many machete wielding martial artists as they can rustle up."

"Yeah, but first they have to find me." Bolan considered the map of French Guiana he'd pinned to the wall.

Kurtzman scanned his notes. "What about this French agent, Erulin?"

"She's a real wild card. I'll have to play that one by ear. It may well backfire, and I already missed today's dinner date at the café."

"So she's probably pissed off at you, as well." Kurtzman shook his head ruefully. "Have you made any friends down south?"

"Actually, Marmion and Ilyanov are probably my best bets as allies. They don't like me, but they know they have a problem."

"So what are you going to do?"

"Gunung and the two shooters are our best lead. I'm afraid I'm going to have to give him another shot at me. The contacts he has at the Jungle Warfare School will have told them I made an appearance and spoke with the commandant and Ilyanov. If I stick my head out, they have no choice but to take a shot at it."

"Great." Kurtzman clearly didn't like the plan. "Another suicide run. You know—"

"Bear," Bolan interrupted. "Hold on a minute."

A red light blinked into life on a small black box plugged into Bolan's computer. His security suite at the bungalow was rudimentary at best. He had spiked four small motion sensors in the shrubbery at each corner of the house.

The one facing the river was blinking in alarm.

Bolan flicked the Beretta 93-R's selector switch to 3-round burst. The sound suppressor was already in place and the magazine loaded. "Bear, I'm going to have to get back to you."

"Striker—!"

Bolan closed the computer. He left the light of the bedroom and eased himself into the gloom of the kitchen. The Executioner paused, listening, while his eyes adjusted. He could hear the wind blowing the curtains in the little living room that opened onto the patio facing the water.

Bolan had closed and locked the glass doors.

There was a minute click, and the sound of the wind ceased as someone closed the doors.

The soldier moved silently back into the bedroom and made his way to the bathroom. He eased open the narrow window over the sink and quickly slid himself outside. His feet made no noise as he landed catlike in the dirt. Only one sensor had gone off, but that did not mean there weren't more enemies in the darkness. Bolan hugged the shadows as he doubled back toward the patio. Moonlight shone down through the trees, and there were wet spots on the patio bricks.

His enemy had come up out of the river. Bolan

scanned the glistening trail and determined one person had made it.

Bolan eased open the glass doors as he ghosted his opponent.

Through the kitchen and down the hallway the light in the bedroom flicked off.

Bolan suspected Kurtzman had just been kidnapped. He moved slowly into the kitchen and eased himself toward the door to the hallway.

He threw himself to one side as the ruby red dot of a laser sight swept along the doorjamb toward his head. He heard the sound of a silenced pistol cycling, and a piece of the door violently broke away. The Beretta chuffed three times in response as Bolan rolled into the breakfast nook and took himself out of the line of fire.

The Executioner's nostrils flared as he smelled the sharp stink of burned high explosive.

He spun the suppressor off the Beretta's threaded barrel. Waking up the neighbors was no longer his biggest consideration. It was time to give the enemy something to worry about. He considered the angle of the shot that had hit the doorway. The enemy was very likely wearing night-vision goggles.

Bolan snaked his arm around the door frame and squeezed the Beretta's trigger. The hallway strobed with muzzle-flash as the machine pistol ripped off three rounds. The Beretta hammered in Bolan's hand as he pumped bursts down the hall. A single tiny flare of high explosive smashed paint and wood above Bolan's arm in response. He fired two more bursts and ejected his empty magazine. He slid in a fresh one as he heard movement in the bedroom.

Bolan came around the corner firing. He ran down

the hallway and rolled as he came through the bedroom door. He came up and the corner of the bed near
his head popped like a firecracker. Bolan could dimly
see his opponent by the bathroom door. He shoved the
Beretta out with both hands and pumped a 3-round
burst into the center body mass. The assassin jerked, but
the ruby beam of his laser tracked and the weapon
clicked twice.

Bolan's opponent was wearing armor.

Something punched into Bolan's soft body armor
below his collarbone. Orange light flared, and bits of un-
burned high-explosive grit blasted into his jaw and
cheek. He jerked his head aside as the ruby beam played
for his face. Bolan raised his aim, and both he and his
opponent went for the head shot. The Beretta snarled
off a burst, and his opponent fell through the bathroom
door.

Bolan rose as the door slammed and the lock clicked.

The Executioner vaulted the bed and fired a dia-
mond pattern of bursts to fill the small cube of space
with lead. He put his foot into the flimsy door, which
smashed back on its hinges.

The bathroom was empty and the window was open.

Bolan charged back through the house. He passed
the bed and found his computer had indeed been hi-
jacked. He reached into his pocket and pulled out his
key chain. Bolan flung open the glass doors of the living room and ran out onto the patio. He could barely
see his opponent moving at a dead run for the river.

Bolan raised his key chain.

It looked like the small, black plastic case for an auto
alarm. Bolan pushed the three buttons in sequence. A
flare of high explosive popped out in the dark. It was a

small charge, designed to permanently destroy the laptop's hard drive and all data it contained. The runner stumbled as the computer exploded in his hands. Bolan sprinted after the staggering figure. The Beretta cycled in his hands as he pumped burst after burst into the fleeing assassin's back.

The killer belly flopped into the river.

Bolan skidded to the bank and pumped the rest of his magazine into the moonlit ripples of the assassin's wake. The Executioner reloaded and watched the surface of the water. The ripples slowly faded, and the river resumed its sluggish, starlit calm.

The assassin was either dead at the bottom or had an air bottle.

Bolan wasn't betting on death. He waited long minutes, but nothing disturbed the water and there was no sound save the whine of the mosquitoes rising to the smell of his sweat and the blood on his face.

The soldier turned and walked back toward the house. He stopped and picked for a moment through the shattered remnants of his computer. His head turned at a gleam a few feet away in the grass.

He picked up a pistol.

The grip had the contoured ergonomic shape of a target pistol. A laser sight was fitted beneath the barrel. A sound suppressor was threaded onto the muzzle. Bolan thrust the gun under his belt and went back to the house.

It seemed his cover was blown just about everywhere.

9

The Executioner was fairly sure Jolie Erulin was wearing soft body armor at the moment. He'd had no choice but to return to Cayenne after the night attack. Bolan was not surprised to see Erulin sitting at the café when he arrived.

"I believe one of your boys is a traitor," Bolan said in greeting.

Erulin's smile went dead on her face. "Fuck you."

Bolan reached into his jacket and pulled out the laser-sighted, Unique D.E.S 32U pistol his unsuccessful assassin had dropped. He put it on the table between them. "Mean anything to you?"

She stared very long and hard at the weapon. "Where did you get this?"

"Someone was shooting that very pistol at me last night, in the city of Roura." Bolan shrugged. "Not exactly foreign legion issue."

"No. It is not."

"So, someone gave a legionnaire the weapon or someone took the liberty of doing the job themselves."

Erulin glared. "What are you implying?"

"I'm just wondering about your little pals Roland and Alain."

"Well, you beat the shit out them." The French agent tossed her head. "They would love to break your legs, but kill you? No. Plus, they have specific orders to leave you alone until I tell them otherwise."

"That's very reassuring," Bolan said. "But what if they have higher motivations than personal vengeance?"

"You mean being Muslim terrorists?" Erulin regarded Bolan dryly. "Alain and Roland are both good Catholic boys and enjoy their jobs. I cannot imagine them being mixed up with Muslim terrorists, much less my not knowing about it. For that matter, I know for a fact that before they were assigned to the South American sector they had killed such people without remorse. Indeed, you might say with pleasure."

Bolan turned his icy glare on the woman. "And you?"

Her laugh surprised Bolan. "Yours is an amusing accusation."

"How is that?"

"Because I am Jewish." She rolled her eyes in bemusement. "You know, usually, I am suspected of aiding and abetting Israeli Intelligence, not their enemies. That is one reason why I am usually assigned to the South American or South Pacific sectors. Here my actions and motivations are not suspect as they might be in Paris or the Middle East."

"That still leaves me with an unidentified shooter with one of your guns."

"Yes." Her face fell again. "You are not a bringer of glad tidings."

"I'm sorry, but the problem was here long before I was."

"Yes." She stared at Bolan steadily. "It was."

"So what have your superiors said about speaking with me?"

The woman took a long sip of her coffee. "I am to use my best judgment, without compromising the national interests of France."

"That's reasonable enough. So what do you know about the terrorist menace in French Guiana?"

"Very little. We did not believe we had one until very recently. We had rumors, coming from our Middle East sector, that something was happening here. We were fairly certain it had something to do with the Javanese in Suriname, but the trail led to Indonesia and then the legion. Other than Caporal-Chef Gunung, we are at a loss for leads."

"And he's currently AWOL."

"Or dead." She raised an eyebrow meaningfully at Bolan. "Word has filtered to us from our agents in Suriname about a gun battle on the Amazonian Highway."

"Ki had a bunch of Javanese assisting him. However, he had two accomplices forming a roadblock. I didn't get a good look at them, but both men were wearing legion pattern Ranger boots and carrying FAMAS rifles. Counting Ki, there are three known Muslims in the Jungle Warfare School at the moment."

"Yes." The French agent frowned. "But Atrache and Sahin were accounted for at the time of the battle in Suriname."

"So it was someone else." Bolan looked at Erulin pointedly. "Are you sure there are no other Muslims at the jungle warfare camp?"

"It is a small establishment. If someone else in the foreign legion were stopping what they were doing five times a day and kneeling toward Mecca, we would know about it."

"There are special dispensations for the five times prayer." Bolan motioned the waitress for some coffee. "One of them is war. Particularly jihad."

Erulin looked at Bolan incredulously. "You are saying that there are terrorist moles in the legion Jungle Warfare School?"

"You're saying Atrache and Sahin were accounted for during the fight in Suriname," Bolan countered. "So who were the shooters at the roadblock?"

Erulin's teeth bit into the fullness of her lower lip. Nothing Bolan had to say was making her happy. "All right, let's work with that hypothesis. What do they intend? Besides having talented goons at their disposal, why go to the trouble of infiltrating the legion? If they need them, they can call on foot soldiers from across the globe. The foreign legion, on the other hand, is one of the most exclusive military organizations in the world. The discipline is savage, and as for subverting soldiers or infiltrating them, it would be an almost useless exercise. Legionnaires are not allowed to leave France or French territories except when they are on training missions or extremely special leave. It would be just about the worst military group in the world to attempt to infiltrate and form cadres of terrorists. They have no opportunity to act."

"Ki managed to go walkabout," Bolan said.

"Yes. He did, but to what point? What possible target could terrorists have in French Guiana?"

Bolan smiled and drank coffee. He was beginning to form his own ideas. "You tell me. What possible target could Muslim terrorists have in French Guiana?"

Erulin's knuckles whitened around her coffee cup. "The satellite launch facility at Kourou."

"I gather you've stepped up security?"

"*We* have not. It is not in Action Direct's purview. However, we have made our recommendations, and security at Kourou has been doubled, and that may be part of the problem."

Bolan raised an eyebrow. "How so?"

"The French foreign legion is in charge of security at the launch center."

Bolan began to feel a distinct sinking feeling in his stomach. "Perhaps I should speak with your superiors."

"Yes, perhaps that would be best." Erulin scooped up her cigarettes as Bolan rose and dropped some money on the table. It had been a sunny morning, but a tropical rain began as they walked outside. "Listen, you must tell me more about you before I can—"

Erulin jerked as if she had taken a blow and fell backward into Bolan's arms. He went with the fall and rolled as the windowpane behind him shattered.

There were snipers on the roof across the street.

Bolan rolled through the rain-abandoned tables and chairs as he drew the 93-R. A wrought-iron table jerked and twisted near his skull. The Beretta tore into life as Bolan returned fire. Two men were on the opposite roof with telescopic rifles. The barrels of their weapons were fat with the black tubes of sound suppressors. The table jerked and skidded with a second rifle shot. Bolan ignored it and put his front sight on the silhouette of the shooter. His 3-round burst struck man and rifle, and the assassin fell back out of view.

Thunder exploded on the street.

Erulin was up, and she held a Colt Delta Elite firmly with both hands. A stream of the vilest obscenities in the French language sizzled off her lips as the massive stainless-steel pistol hammered in her hands.

The Beretta ripped chips out of the roof across the street as Bolan fired burst after burst.

The second sniper dropped out of sight as he faded back across the rooftop.

People on the streets and inside the restaurant were screaming.

Erulin glared at the opposite roof and ejected her spent magazine. "Fuckers…"

She swayed as raindrops sizzled on her smoking, empty pistol. Her knees buckled as she fumbled for a fresh clip, and the French agent sat down hard on the wet tiles. Bolan grabbed her by the shoulders and dragged her behind cover inside. There was a ragged hole torn in the front of her jacket. Buttons popped as Bolan ripped open her blouse. The copper base of a rifle bullet protruded out of her soft body armor directly over her heart. She was very lucky the enemy had been using suppressed, subsonic ammunition. She had taken one hell of a bodyshot.

Bolan finished reloading Erulin's pistol for her and pressed it into her hands. "Can you walk?"

"I think so." She let out a moan as he pulled her to her feet. "Where should we go?"

"Not back to your headquarters," Bolan said.

"Pick a place." She sagged against him. "Random."

"Random it is." Bolan took most of her weight as they moved through the gawking restaurant patrons and went out the back. He put her on the back of his bike and jumped into the saddle. "Hold on tight."

"Where are we going to go?"

Bolan checked his mental map. "West."

"What is west?"

The Executioner gunned the Ducati's engine. He was going to have to lose the bike. He would miss it, but he had attracted all the necessary attention for the moment. It was time to go stealth.

"What is west?" Erulin asked again.

Bolan spoke over his shoulder as he whipped the bike out of the alley and onto the street. "The satellite launch facility at Kourou."

10

Bolan opened his eyes.

The light of dawn coming through the drapes had painted the room a soft pink. Jolie Erulin was snoring, but so softly it was charming. Her left breast had a remarkable purple bruise over her heart.

Bolan had rendered what aid and comfort he could.

He spoke very softly. "You're snoring. Roll over."

She rolled over and mumbled in half-conscious French. "You're a pig."

Bolan grinned and rolled out of the bed. He took his new laptop and satellite rig off of the bedstand and went to the bathroom. He left the door open as he lowered the toilet seat cover and sat with the laptop across his knees. Bolan's eyes stayed on the beautiful woman as he punched keys and then put in his earpiece.

Kurtzman's slightly distorted face blinked onto the screen and he spoke in Bolan's ear. "You're typing, not talking. Are you in danger, or just using discretion?"

"Both," Bolan typed. He craned the little camera attached to the laptop on its flexible neck and pointed it at the bed.

Kurtzman's eyes widened. "Um…wow. Is that an ally or the opposition?"

Bolan considered that carefully. "Don't know. Haven't decided. Don't know if she has, either. We got hammered outside a café about twenty-four hours ago. I got some help from Kiraly's contacts. I sent the Cowboy a .30-caliber rifle bullet I pulled out of Jolie's armor. Any data back?"

"He got it." Kurtzman punched keys and a picture appeared in the corner of Bolan's screen. The rifle depicted was very futuristic looking, with a skeletal frame, a telescopic sight and an adjustable folding stock and bipod. A long black suppressor tube shrouded the rifle's barrel. "That look like what they were pointing at you?"

"Couldn't swear to it. First instinct is yes," Bolan typed.

"Well, it'll probably come as no surprise, but it's French. A PGM. They call it the UR, or Ultima Ratio."

Bolan smiled as he typed. "The Last Argument."

"That's the one. The Cowboy could determine by the rifling and by the marks that it was subsonic, but if you dug it out of Miss Erulin's armor and she was still breathing, you probably already figured that out."

"The French foreign legion is responsible for base security at the satellite launch facility at Kourou."

"I found that out myself a little while ago. Kind of an ugly twist to the plot," Kurtzman replied.

"That's the question," Bolan typed. "What's the plot? France is a whole lot more popular in the Middle East than we are. Even when they were part of the coalition during Desert Storm, Paris was cutting their own deals with Baghdad. We're the Great Satan, I find it hard to believe that al Qaeda or anyone else of their ilk would want to stage a terrorist attack in French Guiana. The few space shots that the Muslim states have had anything to do with go up from here."

"It's a conundrum all right. I really don't see how there are enough legionnaires in French Guiana to launch an assault on the base, and even if they manage to plant a bomb from the inside or blow up a rocket on the pad, so what? Where's the payoff?"

"I don't know. I'm going to the launch facility." Bolan glanced at the woman on the bed. "I'm betting if I ask real nice, Jolie can get me a tour a few levels higher than the usual tourist walk through."

Guiana Space Center, Kourou

IT WAS A VERY impressive facility.

The clearance badge Erulin wore covered the bullet hole in her suit jacket. She had gotten the clearances within two hours, and whatever was written on them in numbers and French got them through the front gates and past the guards with salutes all around.

The guards at the gate and around the perimeter had all been French foreign legionnaires.

They drove to a huge white building flying the French flag. Gleaming glass doors hissed open and blessedly air-conditioned air swept over them. The massive arc of a circular reception desk faced the doors. A beautiful young Creole woman in a blue jacket smiled at them brightly as they entered. She spoke in rapid French to Erulin but kept her eyes on Bolan. She turned her smile up to full wattage as she addressed him in very thick English.

"Would you care for coffee or tea? Dr. Poulain is on his way down."

"Nothing." Bolan smiled. "Thank you."

The doors behind the desk hissed open.

The director of the Guiana space center was a short,

bald and exceptionally energetic looking man in his late fifties. He wore an impeccably tailored gray suit and as he walked into the room his personality preceded him.

Sergent-Chef Vasily Ilyanov walked through the doors at the director's side. He was in full ceremonial legion tropical uniform. The Russian sergeant's Beretta pistol was strapped to his hip.

Bolan noticed the Russian carried his pistol cocked.

The director walked up and kissed Erulin on the cheeks. He turned and stuck out his hand to Bolan. He spoke excellent English.

"Good morning, my friend! I received word from Paris just an hour ago that we were having guests. It is a pleasure to meet you, Mr...." The director raised a questioning eyebrow as his voice trailed off.

Bolan took the hand and shook it. The Director had a strong grip. "Cooper. Thank you for seeing us. Do I call you Director or Dr. Poulain?"

"You could call me either, but I would prefer you called me Bernard."

"Call me Matt." On instinct Bolan liked the man. "I hope we're not interrupting your schedule."

The director let his eyes rove over Erulin. "A man would have to be insane or blind not to interrupt his schedule for Miss Erulin, and as for interrupting my schedule, I am so often in Paris cleaning up messes and taking meetings that I miss most of the launches here." The director's smile turned conspiratorial. "And to be honest, with the schedule I keep, I only rarely get the opportunity to show people my toys."

Bolan matched the director's cunning smile. "And your security has been doubled, and no one will tell you anything."

Both Erulin and Ilyanov shot Bolan arch looks.

Dr. Poulain only laughed. "Indeed, I shall play the three of you against one another and hopefully learn something useful. Meanwhile, all of you, please follow me."

They followed the director into the elevator and began ascending.

"You have a launch scheduled soon?" Bolan asked.

"Indeed. Within the week." The doors hissed open and they found themselves stepping into an observation lounge. Gigantic windows that curved up into the ceiling faced the airstrip and the two launch pads. There was also a well-appointed bar. The director waved at the young man behind it. "Champagne for our guests," he ordered.

Bolan went up to one of the windows and gazed out across the facility. The two launch pads sat more than a mile away. One was empty. On the other the gleaming white spire of a rocket towered toward the noon sun. Technicians looked like ants as they serviced and prepared the spacecraft.

Bolan admired the clean lines of the rocket. "The Ariane-5. It's beautiful," he said.

"Indeed, she is. She carries twenty-five tonnes of liquid oxygen and twenty-five tonnes of liquid hydrogen! She is capable of carrying out multiple restarts and will be powerful enough to put a dual payload of twelve tonnes into a geostationary transfer orbit."

"Twelve tonnes." Bolan nodded respectfully.

Ilyanov gazed out the window. His blue eyes regarded the rocket intently. A glass of champagne was untouched in his hand. "In Russia, we have much larger, but nothing so elegant."

Poulain was clearly pleased. "And you, Jolie?"

Agent Erulin peered out the window briefly. "Three grown men ogling a rocket. I am sure Freud would have something to say."

Poulain threw back his head and laughed.

The door to the lounge opened, and three more people entered the room. Poulain smiled. "Ah, Monsieur Cooper, may I introduce Dr. Guy Dutronc, my second in command, and the man who really runs this facility."

Bolan shook hands with another bald, beaming, French rocket scientist.

"And may I introduce Dr. Babu Seth, our payload engineer."

Dr. Seth had a head of hair Albert Einstein would have envied. He was clearly Indian and spoke English with an Oxford accent. "Pleased to meet you."

Poulain's already warm smile grew warmer as he gestured at the third scientist. "And of course, our jewel."

The woman wore a white lab coat, but neither that, the square framed glasses, nor her severely pulled back black hair could hide the fact that she was very beautiful. Her gray eyes regarded Bolan neutrally as she extended her hand.

Poulain noted Bolan's approval and grinned. "May I introduce Dr. Feresteh Mohammedkhani."

Alarm bells went off in Bolan's head. He smiled and took the scientist's hand. "That's a beautiful name. Is it Persian?" he asked.

The woman's carefully neutral expression warmed slightly. One corner of her generous mouth turned up. "Yes, and thank you."

"She is the true rocket scientist here," Poulain

gushed. "It is largely because of her that our rocket is ahead of schedule and even more powerful than the original design specifications."

"I'm pleased to make your acquaintance. I understand you have a launch coming up," Bolan said.

"Yes." Dr. Mohammedkhani's eyes strayed to the window. "The launch is scheduled for the end of the week."

"What are you sending up?"

"Oh, just a little something in the name of France," Poulain interrupted. Seth and Dutronc both laughed. Poulain shrugged. "As to its exact nature and capabilities, you would have to speak with Dr. Seth, and I apologize, but it will take more than having Miss Erulin on your arm to speak of the current payload. I am afraid it would take a phone call from a certain department in Paris that I have yet to receive."

Bolan nodded. "So this is strictly a French launch."

"Yes, this particular launch is strictly a French launch, and a strictly classified one."

Bolan accepted the statement. "Some sort of satellite, I suppose," he said.

"So one might suppose," Poulain agreed vaguely.

"Anything terrorists might be interested in?"

Dr. Mohammedkhani rolled her eyes. Whatever goodwill Bolan had earned in the last two minutes was clearly crushed. Seth and Dutronc looked openly dubious.

Poulain frowned deeply. "It is not a weapon, I can assure you. To my knowledge, the nation of France has never had in the past nor has any current or future plans to field hypervelocity rail guns or orbiting X-ray laser battle stations." He looked at Bolan pointedly. "Those are projects only the United States has the political and economic wherewithal to consider."

Bolan met Poulain's critical stare. "I was not implying that France is secretly deploying space weapons, Dr. Poulain."

"No." The director relented. "You were not. At the risk of breaching security, I will tell you what you already suspect. My rocket carries an observation satellite. A highly sophisticated one. One with technologies that yours or any other government would be highly interested in obtaining. Those technologies are highly classified. Just who, what, or in what manner the satellite is designed to make its observations is also highly classified. Now, I suppose any observation satellite might be used in tracking terrorist activities in one form or another. However, I must express grave doubts as to this satellite being any kind of viable target for a terrorist attack. For that matter, if terrorists truly wished to attack the European Space Center, the liquid fuel production facility would make a much better target. We produce liquid hydrogen, oxygen and other highly volatile compounds in vast quantities there. It is only a few kilometers from here. A single, well-placed bomb would produce multiple, spectacular, fuel-air explosions, killing hundreds if not thousands here at the space facility and do untold damage."

"Still, the destruction of a French spy satellite, with an explosion on the pad, it would make headlines, and be a blow to French prestige."

"I suppose," Poulain agreed. "However, this is an unmanned rocket. A French rocket blowing up in French Guiana would hardly spur an international furor, even if terrorists were suspected. We would simply tighten security and continue with our scheduled launches, and people like Miss Erulin and her shadowy associates would hunt down the perpetrators and kill them."

Bolan looked out across the field toward the gleaming rocket. He was grasping at straws, and he knew it. He also knew there was a piece of the puzzle here. His every instinct told him he was on the right track. "There's something going on here in French Guiana."

"I am sure there is. I knew it must be so when Jolie contacted me this morning. Hardly any man in French Guiana is lucky enough to entertain her without national security being somehow involved. I have spent the entire morning trying to figure out what kind of plot there might be." Poulain put a friendly hand on Bolan's shoulder. "As I have mentioned, I believe the liquid-fuel production facility would be the most viable target. However, security has been doubled both there and throughout the entire spaceport. Sergent-Chef Ilyanov could tell you more of it, but I am assured that the legionnaires have the wherewithal to destroy a truck bomb long before it comes close to any significant building. Airspace is also strictly controlled around Kourou."

Bolan glanced at Ilyanov. He suspected there were rockets secreted around Kourou. Rockets small enough for a man to fire from his shoulder. That, in itself, offered a new form of attack, and one from within.

Ilyanov read Bolan's mind. "All legionnaires of the Muslim faith with guard duties at the spaceport have been temporarily reassigned."

Dr. Mohammedkhani went rigid. Her face flushed, but her gray eyes were glacial as they regarded first Ilyanov and then Bolan. She spun on her heel without a word and stormed out of the lounge.

The Frenchmen all shrugged and sipped more champagne.

It was a sensible precaution, but Poulain was right. One unmanned rocket carrying an observation satellite in French Guiana didn't have much cachet as a terrorist target. There was a bigger threat. Bolan knew it. It was close enough to smell.

But he couldn't identify it.

Poulain's shoulders sagged defeatedly. "I am sorry, my friend." He brightened slightly. "But it would be my pleasure to give you a personally guided tour."

"I'd like that," the Executioner said.

"I THINK HE LIKED YOU." Erulin pulled away from the space center in the ancient, rented Peugeot.

"I liked him, too. I respect any man who is passionate about what he does." Bolan smiled. "Dr. Poulain seemed awfully fond of you, as well."

The French agent ran her eye up and down Bolan as she drove. "I like men who are passionate about what they do, as well." She shrugged as she lit a cigarette. "Also, Action Direct is partly responsible for security at Kourou, but only in an intelligence-gathering role. Bernard, I mean Dr. Poulain, and I have…worked together, on several occasions."

"What do you know about Dr. Mohammedkhani?" Bolan asked.

Erulin's cigarette dipped in her mouth as her lips quirked. "She's pretty, I suppose."

Bolan grinned. "I didn't know you were the jealous type."

"I am. Never forget that."

"I won't. Get her phone number and address for me."

She took her eyes off the road and leveled a gaze at Bolan. "You are a pig."

Bolan laughed.

Erulin punched up data on her personal organizer and scribbled information on an old receipt while at the same time driving with her knees and somehow lighting another cigarette. She handed Bolan the scrap of paper. "Here. Good luck. She hates you. I can tell."

"Love and hate." Bolan held up his thumb and fore-finger an inch apart. "This close."

Erulin smirked.

"I need to contact home. You can drop me off at the café near the hotel," Bolan said.

"I also need to contact my superiors, preferably without you about. We'll meet back at the room in say, an hour? And compare notes?"

"It's a date."

They drove the few miles back into town, and Erulin brought the car to a screeching halt. Bolan took the suitcase containing his laptop and satellite rig and went into the café. He took a table near the rear exit and put his back to the wall as he connected. A bartender brought Bolan coffee.

Kurtzman blinked onto the screen. "So how was the spaceport?"

"Interesting. They could teach NASA a few tricks. Could an Ariane-5 reach the United States?"

"You mean ballistically, like a missile?" Kurtzman snorted. "The Ariane-5 was designed to take satellites up into high, low and medium Earth orbits. It could easily reach any point in the U.S., including Hawaii and Alaska."

Bolan had suspected as much. "So what do you think?"

"As a terrorist threat? It looks gorgeous on paper, and I've already considered that one. First you'd have to switch the guidance package, not inconceivable, but the minute anyone runs any kind of check, which they do about a thousand times before liftoff, the cat's going to be out of the bag."

"What if you've got that covered?" Bolan glanced at the piece of paper with the number and the address in his hand. "What if you have someone high up on the inside. In the control room?"

"Well, that would be a feat in of itself, but just for argument's sake, I'll give it to you. So you switch the guidance package, you find a loose nuke, and you load her up and blast her off in a great big perfect arc and Washington, D.C., is ground zero. You have one last, and in my opinion, insurmountable hurdle."

Bolan sipped coffee. "Reentry."

"Right!" Kurtzman grinned proudly at Bolan. "The Ariane-5 is a one-way ticket. It's designed to take things up, not bring them back down. It could make the first part of the journey without breaking a sweat, but coming back down, its payload would burn up in the high atmosphere long before it even got close to its target. To get past that, you would have to design a special reentry vehicle for your weapon, sneak it into the space center, fool every single technician involved in assembly and mounting into thinking it's the correct payload, and remember, it will look nothing like the satellite it is replacing. It would look different, it would mount different, and your takeoff weight would change. You would raise red flags every step of the way with the lowliest technicians to the highest level engineers controlling the project, and like I said, everything is checked, thousands of times, right up to takeoff. To make it happen, you would literally have to control the entire facility. Top to bottom."

Bolan frowned into the middle distance.

Kurtzman nodded. "And I've taken it down that route. All the way down to the last permutation. Let's say every single French foreign legionnaire in French Guiana converts to Islam and they take the spaceport. And they have the scientists in place and lined up to switch the payloads. That rocket would still never leave the launch pad. If the spaceport were taken, France would assault it. Mirage VI supersonic strategic bombers could cross the Atlantic in about two and a half hours and destroy anything on either of the two launch pads." Kurtzman scratched his head. "For that matter, worst-case scenario, the spaceport has been taken, the rocket is modified, and we are sixty minutes and counting to Armageddon, the French could pull a Final Option of their own and nuke the facility from one of their subs in the Pacific. I'm sorry, Striker, but the Ariane-5 just doesn't work as a terrorist weapon."

"Do me a favor anyway." Bolan typed in the name, number and address from the paper he held. "Find me everything you can on a Dr. Feresteh Mohammedkhani, currently working for the French national space program in French Guiana. I believe she's Iranian, probably immigrated to France and went to university at the Polytechnical School. Her specialty is rocket design."

"I'm on it. What are you going to do, meanwhile?"

"I don't know. I think Jolie knows more than she's

telling me, but not much. I'm going to buy her lunch and see if her superiors have cleared her to tell me anything interesting. By that time, I'm hoping you'll have something on Dr. Mohammedkhani, and I'll pay her a visit."

"Contact me in two hours. I'll see what I can do."

"Striker out." Bolan closed up the link and finished his coffee. An afternoon rainstorm broke out and beat down on the streets. People in the streets ducked into doorways. Bolan jogged across the street to the hotel. Inside, the man at the front desk gestured to him.

Bolan caught the disturbed look in the man's eyes and his hand crept toward the concealed Beretta 93 R. "Yes?"

"Your…lady friend. She is gone."

"Gone?" Bolan locked eyes with the man. "Where?"

The man flinched. "I do not know, sir. But she looked very unhappy, and was in the company of a number of very unpleasant looking men. I almost called the police."

"What kind of men?"

"Javanese I suspect, and rough looking. One of them had very frightening eyes, I…" The man's eyes bugged as the machine pistol appeared in Bolan's hand. The soldier took the stairs three at a time to the second-story landing. He went down the hall and could see that the door to his room was standing open. Bolan flicked his selector switch to 3-round-burst mode and went through the door.

There was no sign of a struggle, save for a Colt Delta Elite lying unfired on the carpet. Bolan lowered his pistol as he stared at the bedstand. The twelve-inch snake-curved blade of a kris was sunk into the wood.

The blade impaled a piece of paper. Only four words were written on it. The words were written in English.

"Leave or she dies."

11

Cayenne

"Everything is going according to plan."

"Everything was going according to plan before. You said the American was a hunted man, and there was nowhere he could hide from the legion." Babar looked askance at the Commander. "So he went to the legion camp and made friends with the commanding officer."

"Yes…" The Commander regarded Babar dryly until the giant broke eye contact. "This American does appear to very resourceful."

Cigarette spoke. "You think kidnapping the woman is enough to draw him off?"

"No, I do not believe so. Not at all. But that was never really my intention. The way this man is, he will act. It will be his undoing."

"But what about his allies?" Babar inquired. It was clear the giant would not be satisfied until he had personally pulled the American's head from his shoulders. "He keeps calling upon resources he should not be able to use. As I said, he has made war against the legion, yet somehow acquired the cooperation of the commandant of the Jungle Warfare School."

The Commander smiled again. "I am counting on it."

Babar blinked.

"We have contacts in the French foreign legion, do we not?" the Commander chided.

Babar smiled.

"And we have at least one contact I can think of in Action Direct, no?"

Babar smiled to reveal his gold teeth.

"And we have contacts in the local police," the Commander finished. "Babar, my friend, I am counting on our American calling on whatever resources he can muster. He knows he cannot find the woman alone. He will have to seek help. The minute he goes to the legion, we will know it. The minute he contacts Action Direct headquarters, we will know it. The minute he contacts the local police, we will know it."

Cigarette stubbed out his smoke. "Should we go and insure it?"

"No, not yet. The trap is set. When he makes his move, as I say, we will know it. All our accomplices need is five minutes' warning, and they will be ready for him."

"Yes," Babar said. "But what about us? I think Cigarette is right. We need to take this matter firmly into our own hands."

"Do you know something?" the Commander asked. "I agree. We will assemble the strike team. We get the word when he moves. When he moves, we do. We will let him walk into the trap."

"And we will be outside waiting." Babar grinned. "Should he once more prove himself resourceful."

"Exactly." The Commander's eyes burned as he looked into the American's short and brutal future.

Guiana Space Center

"WE HAVE a problem."

Dr. Poulain nearly jumped out of his shoes as Bolan materialized behind him in the parking lot. He sagged against the door of his Mercedes clutching his chest. "You nearly made me change my pants, my friend."

"I'm sorry, Doctor, but it was necessary to speak to you alone."

"Just what sort of problem do we have? Have you discovered something new?"

Bolan shook his head. "Jolie has been kidnapped."

"Kidnapped?" Poulain's face fell. "By whom?"

"Terrorists. The ones I tracked to French Guiana. They want me to break off my investigation."

"But, you must—"

"I can't, and I won't." Bolan's face was grim. "Jolie's probably already dead, or wishes she was, and even if I leave and break off my investigation, even if they let her go, she won't break off hers. They'll have to kill her anyway."

"So…a rescue." Dr. Poulain's jaw suddenly set. "Or revenge."

"Those are the only viable options."

Poulain nodded. "I will contact Ilyanov, he will—"

"I would rather you didn't do that."

"But…" The scientist shook his head. "Ilyanov is a foreign legion commando, he can—"

"The activities of the French foreign legion have been compromised." Bolan's voice was stone. "So have those of Action Direct, and I don't know just exactly how bad it is or how far up the chain it runs."

Poulain's eyes hardened. "I keep a pistol in my car, and I have a shotgun at home. What is it you propose?"

Bolan smiled grimly. The little rocket scientist seemed to be in deadly earnest. "I'd like you to get on the phone. Jolie has at least one team that I know of working under her, two men—"

"Roland Aretos and his partner, Alain Reno. I do not know them well. However, when Jolie returned to France for a month last year, she gave me the phone number of the big one, Roland, to call in case there was some kind of intelligence crisis at the space center. I have met him a few times, socially. Alain is relatively new. I have seen him assigned to visiting dignitaries as part of security. Other than that, I do not know much about them."

Neither did Bolan. "Gut instinct, do you trust them?"

"Roland struck me as a brutal man." Poulain nodded slowly. "But I do not doubt his loyalty to France, or to Jolie. Alain I simply do not know."

It would have to be enough. "Call Roland. Tell him you have an intelligence emergency. Don't tell him what kind, and tell him that you can't talk over the phone. Tell him to meet you at your house immediately."

"You drive." Dr. Poulain pulled handed Bolan his keys. He took out his cell phone and began searching its address book for the number. Bolan revved the engine as Poulain began speaking rapidly into the phone in French. The doctor suddenly stopped talking and listened for several minutes as Bolan drove toward town. Poulain lowered the phone and looked over at Bolan. "Aretos says he will meet you at my house. He is in Kourou. He says he can be there in five minutes."

Bolan did the math. The facility was out and away from the city, and it would take him ten minutes breaking every speed limit. He had wanted to be the one waiting, but the cards had been dealt and would have to be played as is. "All right."

Poulain punched the hold button. "Aretos says he already knows."

Bolan scowled. That wasn't good. "How?"

"He did not say. He says you and I are to come alone. He says you are to come unarmed." Poulain shrugged fatalistically. "Will you meet him? Or do you have another plan?"

"You said you keep a pistol in your car?"

"Yes." Poulain opened up his glove box and pulled out a French 1935A. The little pistol was flat, lustrously blued and had elegant lines. Bolan had fired one before. They were very accurate, quite reliable, and like all prewar French pistols they were also woefully underpowered.

"You any good with it?" Bolan asked.

"I can keep most rounds in the black at twenty-five meters."

Bolan locked his gaze with the scientist. "Who do you trust more? Me, or Aretos?"

Poulain frowned. "Well, I do not wish to seem a traitor. But I trust you."

"Good. I believe you. There's a good chance this is an ambush. If it comes down to it, give Roland my gun, but keep yours in your pocket. Stand close to them. If you have to shoot, shoot Roland first. Shoot him twice, once in the body and then once in the head. Then give Alain the same."

Poulain considered this. "Very well." He cocked his pistol and put it into his coat pocket. He took Aretos off hold and told him the meet was a go.

Bolan took out the Beretta 93-R and handed it to the doctor after he clicked the phone shut. Poulain's eyes widened when he saw the machine pistol, and he set it in his lap, They drove for a few minutes in silence until they reached the outskirts of Kourou.

Poulain glanced at the road ahead. "Turn right."

Bolan turned onto a gravel road that paralleled a small river. The road twisted along with the curves of the banks and was lined with tropical trees. Several drives pulled off the road through the trees.

"Many of the engineers keep cottages here." Poulain pointed. "My drive is just ahead."

Bolan pulled onto a short drive that led directly to the river. A small but well-appointed cottage sat at the river's edge with its own pier and speedboat at dock. A black Renault SUV was parked out front. "Is that yours?" Bolan asked.

"No." Poulain shook his head. "They beat us here."

Bolan parked the Mercedes and stepped out. Aretos and Reno immediately appeared from around either side of the house. Each of them carried their weapons in their hands. Poulain stepped out of the car, but the two agents seemed to ignore him. They leveled their pistols at Bolan. "Drop your weapons. Slowly," Aretos said.

Bolan opened his jacket by the corners to show his empty holster. As he did so, the skeleton handle of his boot knife slid into his palm from out of his sleeve. Even wearing soft body armor he doubted he could survive wading through two cylinders of .357 Magnum rounds to get close enough to use it. But the steel was still cold comfort in his hand as he dropped his coat and kept the blade concealed along his wrist. Poulain held up the Beretta by the barrel. "I have his gun. He has come in good faith."

One side of Aretos's single, heavy eyebrows rose slightly. He jerked his head, and Reno took the pistol from the doctor. Poulain stepped back behind the two French agents.

Poulain's right hand slid into his pocket. The Action Direct men took no notice. Bolan had their full attention. Poulain silently drew the pistol and pointed it at the back of Aretos's head.

Aretos's face split into an ugly grin. "I think you have taken an awfully big risk, *mon ami*." He holstered his pistol. "Come on. We are wasting time—"

He turned to find Dr. Poulain putting his own pistol back in his pocket. He whirled and looked back at Bolan dryly. "First you sleep with my boss, now you turn France's leading rocket scientist against me." The big Frenchman shook his head ruefully as he walked into Poulain's cottage. Bolan sheathed his knife and they all followed.

The soldier's eye immediately went to the blood-streaked piece of paper on the coffee table. Aretos sprawled onto the couch. He waved at the note as he lit a cigarette. "This was received a few hours ago."

Bolan picked it up, and he and Poulain both read the note.

"Kill the American. We let her go."

A corner of the bloodstained note had been cut out.

Reno tapped the note with his finger. "It matches Jolie's blood type. A DNA match is being done, but that will take hours even with top priority. We are operating under the assumption that this is for real."

Bolan pulled the note he had received from inside his jacket and handed it to Reno. He grimaced and gave it Aretos. "I gather you are not going to leave?"

"No, and frankly I'm hoping you're not going along with their demands, either."

"No." Aretos's cruel face broke into a smile. "We will kill you when we feel like it. Not at the demand of men who are already dead."

"The question is, where is she?" Reno frowned. "And who has her?"

Bolan took a package wrapped in newspaper from his jacket lining and laid it on the coffee table. Aretos unwrapped it. The three Frenchmen stared at the twelve-inch dagger Bolan had brought with him from the hotel. "Caporal-Chef Ki Gunung has her. You need to run fingerprints on that as soon as possible."

Aretos jerked his head, and Reno rewrapped the dagger and ran out without a word. Aretos glanced back at Bolan. "You are full of surprises. Can you tell us where she is being held, as well?"

Poulain looked at Bolan hopefully.

Bolan had given the matter a great deal of thought. "Ki is a French foreign legion deep reconnaissance commando. If he wants to hide, all he has to do is pull a fade into the jungle. We'll never find him."

Aretos nodded. "Yes, but you do not believe he is hiding."

"No, he's not. He left his calling card, and I suspect the Javanese quarter in Cayenne is small. It won't be too hard to find him."

"You suspect a trap."

"Oh, yeah." Bolan nodded. "A great big one."

"Foolish." Aretos scowled. "What is to prevent me from assembling a strike team and burning him and his little ambush to the ground?"

Bolan sighed. "Action Direct has been compromised."

Aretos glared.

Bolan ignored the Frenchman's anger. There was no way to sugarcoat the situation, and time was short. "They have someone on the inside. The minute you contact headquarters and start assembling your team, someone is going to slip Gunung the word, and he'll disappear. The same will happen if Ilyanov and legion internal security tries anything."

"So we are fucked!" Aretos stabbed out his cigarette angrily. "We sit on our hands and do nothing? Is that what you are saying?"

"No. Action Direct and the legion can't take any kind of action." Bolan shrugged. "But I've got nothing better to do, and I suspect we have an hour or so before the enemy starts to wonder why they can't locate you and Alain. That makes three."

Aretos's ugly smile returned.

"Four." Poulain stepped forward.

Aretos's lip curled derisively. "Put it back in your pants, Doctor."

Poulain was determined. "You need all the help you can get."

"Very well." Aretos's disdain was palpable. "Tell me. Other than getting yourself killed, and my career ruined for losing the leading rocket scientist of France on an unauthorized raid, just what is that you think you can do?"

Poulain didn't back down. "It was a long time ago, but I did my National Service. I was trained as a forward observer, and I know which end of a MAS-49 rifle is which."

Aretos looked at Bolan helplessly.

The soldier shrugged. "He was willing to blow your head off."

"Yes." Aretos glared back at the doctor. "So he was."

Cayenne

ARETOS PULLED Poulain's Mercedes into an alley. The SUV was there, and Reno was waiting. Bolan glanced up as it started to rain. "I need to get some equipment."

"No. You do not leave my sight." Aretos's jaw was set. "You do not disappear. You do not run your own operation. You stick with us, or we put you in the ground like the note said."

Bolan met the Frenchman's stare but detected no deception. Just his own worry and suspicion. The soldier wanted to go to get a full warload of armor and weapons, but he could not afford a fight with his tenuous allies.

This day, it was going to be done the French way.

"We're going to need guns," Bolan said.

The French agent's wolfish smile returned. "That I can do."

They got out into the rain, and Reno popped the hatchback of the Renault. Blankets were piled in the back. Aretos yanked off the top covering.

Bolan stared.

Three 1928 Thompson submachine guns stared back at him.

Aretos shrugged. "They are former Paraguayan police issue. Reported stolen years ago. Untraceable."

Reno took up one of the ancient weapons and inserted a loaded 50-round drum. He gave Bolan his movie-star handsome grin. "Like The Untouchables, no?"

Aretos picked up one of the submachine guns and loaded it. "Do you know which end is which?"

Bolan took up the heavy wood-and-steel weapon. Fully loaded, it was twice as heavy as an M-16. The stock and foregrip were worn, and much of the finish was gone. He racked the action and noted its liquid smoothness. He inserted a drum and racked the action again to load a round. The weapon was well used but had been meticulously maintained. Bolan shook his head. Action Direct agents had a reputation for being cowboys. The reputation was well deserved.

Bolan flipped on the safety. "I'm familiar with it," he said.

Aretos looked derisively at the doctor. "Here." He threw back a blanket and revealed another dinosaur. "Here is your MAS-49."

Poulain took up the battered, old semiautomatic rifle and examined it. He picked up an ancient looking belt of rubberized canvas with six magazine pouches.

Bolan checked the sights on his weapon. It was archaic, but, arguably, it would be harder to think of a better weapon for clearing rooms full of entranced, suicidal Javanese martial artists. Bolan picked up a battered looking gas mask bag that contained two more drums. "Anything else?"

Reno yanked another blanket away to reveal a white plastic five-gallon bucket. It was full to the rim with the brutally knobbed shapes of U.S. military pineapple grenades.

"Argentine army surplus." Aretos began filling his pockets. "Take as many as you want."

Aretos's fist crashed across the man's jaw. "How many?"

The French agent backhanded the Javanese gangster before he could speak, and the man collapsed to the muck of the alley. Reno yanked him up, and Aretos buried his fist into the gangster's guts.

"How many, Munap?" Aretos grinned as the man folded in half and dropped to the ground again. "And where?"

Bolan had been on both ends of some very ugly interrogations. Either way it was a rotten experience. Aretos was enjoying the proceedings just a little too much.

The Javanese quarter in Cayenne was small, and full of immigrants from neighboring Suriname who came to find work as fishermen and dockworkers. Like all immigrants, they brought their gangsters with them. Munap Hubudin had a nasty reputation as a leg breaker, which he backed up with his ancestral martial arts.

A few thousand volts from Reno's stun gun had taken the fight right out of him.

Reno smiled unpleasantly at Bolan. "You want to hit him?"

Bolan was unimpressed. "Hurry up."

"Americans," Reno said. "All business."

Aretos put his foot in Hubudin's crotch and leaned. "Where and how many?"

The gangster winced in agony. His limbs still trembled and twitched from the voltage he'd taken. "I don't know what you're talking about." His voice rose to a shriek as Aretos leaned harder.

"Think," Aretos prompted. "Think very hard. Someone has my boss. I think you know who. Last chance, and then I'm going to stop crushing your balls and I am going to start cutting them."

Reno made a show reloading a fresh pair of probe cartridges into the stun gun. "Maybe he just needs some more juice."

"Or maybe we should just give him to the American." Aretos grinned at Hubudin. "He is all business."

Hubudin's gaze met Bolan's. The gangster's eyes rolled away in terror. "I was told to keep a lookout on the street, and report anything I saw."

Aretos eased up a little bit. "Like what?"

"Police searching the waterfront or asking questions." He glanced at Bolan. "Or strangers."

"Who gave you these orders?" Aretos asked, pressing his foot down.

"Naga!" Munap nearly screamed the name. "Naga!"

Bolan gauged the fear in the man's eyes and saw he was telling the truth. "Who's Naga?" he asked.

"Ngabehi Bagus," Aretos said. "A drug dealer and a pimp. Scum." He took out his handkerchief and wiped Hubudin's blood from his fist. "He has an import-export business, which fronts Guianan marijuana into Europe and then imports heroin. If you want Asian girls, he brings them in from Suriname. He's a small fish, but he rules his own little kingdom in the Javanese quarter. He pays protection to the French syndicates in Paris and pays off the local police regularly. As long as he keeps his crimes in the Javanese community and his dirty work in Suriname, no one bothers him."

Bolan nodded. "Let's go bother him."

Aretos yanked Hubudin to his feet. He shoved his face into the gangster's and grinned like a wolf. "Time to go report, soldier."

12

"Not much on the outside." Aretos stared out the rain-spattered windshield at the corrugated iron wall with a single door. "They say the inside is a veritable pleasure dome." The French agent's face grew ugly as he thought of his boss. "They say the cellars below are a tomb of horrors."

Bolan had seen many such places. Far too many. "What does Naga look like?"

"Short, fat, head like a bullet. Scars under and over his left eye, gold teeth, tattoos. If you see someone who looks like a cartoon character of an Asian gangster, it is Naga."

Bolan had seen far too many of that type, as well. "Let's do it."

Aretos turned to Hubudin and unlocked his handcuffs. "Okay, you're going to go knock on the door. We're going to be right here across the street." He patted the ancient Thompson between his knees. "You screw up, the three of us cut you in two. After we move in, you are allowed to run for your life, and keep running. All the way back to Suriname. Understand?"

The man glanced warily at Bolan. He had met the Executioner's gaze for only a moment, and what he had seen there had left his insides like ice water. He gazed out unhappily at the rain and nodded.

"Good boy." Aretos prodded him with the muzzle of the Thompson. "Now, go."

Hubudin stepped out of the SUV and walked through the rain like a man going to his own funeral. Bolan flicked off the safety of his Thompson and kept the muzzle trained on Hubudin's back. The gangster went up to the door and pressed the button on the intercom. He spoke into it. The rain lashed down against the windshield as they waited.

The door cracked open.

Aretos stomped the accelerator to the floor. The vehicle's tires screamed for traction on the wet cobblestones and then bit down. The SUV tore around in a tight arc and forward for the front door. Hubudin turned and had but a split second to widen his eyes in betrayal and horror as his flesh and bone crumpled under the impact of the grille. The windshield cracked as he went flying over the hood.

Dr. Poulain shouted in alarm as the windshield cracked. The SUV kept going forward. The man who answered the door was smashed back as the frame ripped out of the doorway. Corrugated iron ripped and tore all around the SUV.

The interior of the warehouse was done up like a pasha's palace. Opulent batik prints stretched across the cavernous interior from the ceiling to the floor. The floors were covered with expensive Persian rugs. Carvings of gold, ebony, ivory and jade were everywhere. Potted trees rose to the skylights amid fountains. Bolan had no time to admire the decor. Roland stepped on the brakes. Bolan bolted out of the SUV with his Thompson leveled.

Two Javanese men reclined on cushions smoking a hookah. Half-naked Asian women sat at their feet. The stems of the gangsters' water pipes dangled in their hands. Too late, they reached for the AK-74 rifles by their knees.

A door flung open at the far end of the pleasure dome.

A bald, gold-toothed, scar-faced man who could only be Naga stared slack-jawed at the intruders in his parlor.

Bolan's Thompson roared into life. He hammered both men with 5-round bursts to the chest.

Poulain's rifle cracked twice, but the men were already fallen.

Naga flung the door closed again.

The women screamed and cowered on the ground.

Reno and Aretos held their triggers down, streaming .45-caliber rounds through the door in continuous fire after Naga. Two men with rifles appeared on the balcony above the private room. Bolan raised his aim. He hosed both down before either man got off a shot.

Inside the room, Naga was screaming.

Bolan moved to the door. He stepped to one side and put in a fresh drum as pistols barked from inside the room. The soldier racked his bolt on a fresh round and took a grenade out of his pocket. He nodded at the room as he pulled the pin, and Aretos and Reno began pumping fresh bursts through the walls. The cotter lever pinged away as Bolan opened his hand and then closed it to make a fist around the grenade.

Bolan turned to the door and drove his fist through it.

He opened his hand and dropped the grenade on the

floor within. Someone inside screamed in alarm. There was a crash of furniture within. Bolan drew out his arm and moved away from the door as several bullets smashed outward. He heard the sound of overturning furniture as the grenade detonated with a crack. Bolan turned back and kicked the door in.

A man lay screaming on the floor clutching the ruins of his face. Another bloody, human ruin lay unmoving on the blood-spattered carpets. A huge mahogany desk lay overturned in the corner. There was clearly a man crouching behind it.

Bolan kept his sights on the center of the overturned table. "Come out, Naga."

The gangster rose slowly from behind the table. His left arm hung bloody and useless by his side. He dropped a Colt .45 pistol to the floor and raised his good hand pleadingly as he spoke rapidly in French.

Naga screamed and collapsed as a burst from Reno's gun cut him down at the knees.

Bolan turned. The Frenchmen's weapons were not quite pointing at him. Reno smiled in challenge. His smile was tinged with the sadism Bolan had detected before. He spit in Naga's direction and shrugged. "He's a dead man, anyway. No one fucks with Action Direct, and this starts the interrogation on the right foot."

Dr. Poulain scowled in revulsion as he guarded the door. Bolan went over to where Naga moaned and clutched his legs.

"Tell me where she is, and I won't let them torture you," the Executioner said.

Aretos and Reno lost their smiles.

Dr. Poulain no longer guarded the door. The muzzle of his rifle was now pointing inside the room. Aretos shook his head slowly, but his eyes stayed locked with Bolan as he spoke.

"Poulain...I am going to shove that rifle up your ass."

The scientist brought his rifle to his shoulder and aimed at Aretos. "Try it."

The French agents exchanged a quick glance. Bolan knew they were considering killing him, and possibly the doctor, as well.

Bolan spoke to Naga with grim finality. "Last chance. Before this gets ugly."

"Downstairs! She is alive! Downstairs!"

"Anyone with her?"

"One guard! One guard!" Naga screamed it like a mantra. "One guard!"

Aretos broke eye contact with Bolan. He strode forward and glared at Naga. "You are sure?"

"One guard!"

"Good." Aretos dropped the muzzle of his Thompson onto Naga's chest and squeezed the trigger.

"For God's sake!" Poulain was livid.

Aretos took his time clicking a fresh drum into his weapon, daring Bolan to do something about it. The soldier was not going to buy into the power trip. Yet. He filed the Frenchman away as unfinished business and arranged a smile on his face. "So where's downstairs?"

Aretos glanced around the room. Bolan took over. "Poulain, you stick with me. We'll take the front. Roland, you and Alain take the back. We search every square inch of the place."

The agents began yanking down tapestries and ripping up rugs. Poulain looked thoughtfully at the walls.

Bolan mentally did some math. The building was a converted warehouse. It was a box. The cellar would most likely be new construction. If there were a hidden door rather than a floor hatch there would be an inconsistency in the interior—

"There." Bolan walked across the office. The room was slightly smaller on the inside than it should have been. The carpet was slightly worn in front of one wall section, but there was no visual reason for foot traffic in front of an empty wall. Bolan tapped on the section of wall with his knuckles. He stepped back and put his foot through it.

The panel smashed inward off of its track to reveal a narrow stairwell. Reno pushed forward. He flicked on the light at the top of the stairs and shouted. "Throw down your weapon! Come out! You will not be harmed!"

There was a pause, then an AK-74 rifle clattered at the foot of the stairwell. A man shouted, "Don't shoot!"

A Javanese came up the stairs slowly. He was a big man, but he wasn't Ki. The guard glanced fearfully from muzzle to muzzle of the weapons covering him. Reno drove the barrel of his Thompson into the man's gut as he reached the top and then shoved him to the floor of the office. Aretos patted him down. He tossed the man's knife in a corner. "Poulain, cover him."

Poulain turned his rifle on the man.

"Jolie!" Reno descended the stairs. "Jolie!"

A muffled, though definitely feminine voice came back in answer.

"Jolie!" Reno turned the corner.

The roar of the shotgun was like a stick of dynamite detonating in the confined space. Most of Reno's head was torn away in a hailstorm of lead, brain and bone and splattered the concrete wall behind him. Poulain shouted in alarm and his rifle fired once. Bolan snapped a glance backward. The gangster on the office floor had bounced up like a jumping jack. He had taken one bullet and then kicked the rifle out of Poulain's hands. In the blink of an eye, the Javanese delivered three martial arts hand strikes that drove Poulain to the floor.

Feet pounded in the cellar below.

Bolan dropped his submachine gun and pulled a grenade from his pocket. If the cellar was one room, the woman would be within the lethal fragmentation radius of the grenade. He would have to cut it close. He stepped away from the stairwell as he pulled the pin and waited for the sound of feet hitting the wooden stairs. The wooden stairs groaned, and the cotter lever pinged away as Bolan tossed the grenade and drew his Beretta.

Aretos brought his Thompson to bear as the big Javanese lunged at him. The submachine gun snarled as the grenade down the stairwell detonated. Two bullets smashed into the guard's chest. The weapon fell silent as the man's kick smashed off the Thompson's foregrip and broke Aretos's wrist. The kick continued and bent back the drum at a horrible angle that jammed the feed. The guard's fist pistonned into Aretos's throat, and the French agent fell gagging to the floor.

The gangster spun for Bolan.

The Beretta 93-R drilled a 3-round burst into his chest. Bolan touched off a second and a third burst. Even in a trance, the killer could no longer ignore the damage to his heart and lungs. He stared down stupidly at the bleeding holes in his chest as Bolan raised his aim and finished him with a burst to the head. Bolan whirled on the stairwell as the killer fell.

Ki Gunung flew up out of the stairwell like winged vengeance.

He vaulted the bodies of his two men who had taken the majority of the shrapnel on the narrow stairs. Blood streaked his chest and face, and his empty hands were torn where he had not entirely avoided the flying fragments. Bolan got off one burst as Ki's kick hit him square in the chest. Bolan staggered back. Froth flecked the corners of Ki's mouth, and his eyes rolled back in his head as he spun. The edge of his foot came around in a blinding arc and chopped the 93-R out of Bolan's hand. The Executioner put up his hands to block and the next kick flew in beneath his guard and thundered into his gut. His blocking arm went numb as Ki's next kick tried to crush his skull.

Ki was a martial artist nearly from birth, and he was deep in his trance. Bolan knew he stood no chance in hand-to-hand combat, but he fought on. He stabbed his fingers for Ki's eyes and was rewarded by a deadly kick that missed by inches. Bolan tried to cover as Ki's blows fell like rain. Only the soldier's body armor prevented his ribs from staving in. His arms turned to aching lead as they absorbed the blows meant for his brain.

Ki leaped into the air with a scream. The flying kick took Bolan off his feet and bounced him off the far wall of the office. He forced his brutalized body to move. Ki bent and picked up the dagger on the floor.

Ki stood between the Executioner and the firearms.

Aretos pushed himself up from the floor. His face was a mask of agony as he held his broken wrist up to his throat. His right hand clutched his stun gun. He glared at Ki as the ruby beam of the laser sight whined into life.

Ki turned.

The stun gun chuffed once and then twice as Aretos fired both probes. The barbed darts buried themselves in Ki's chest, and Aretos pumped voltage into Ki's body.

Ki shuddered and jerked as Aretos held down the trigger and drained the battery pack into him. Ki shrieked as he seized the wires and ripped the probes from his body. He closed the gap between himself and Aretos in two strides. Bolan pulled his last grenade from his pocket as he lunged after Ki. Aretos tried to bring up his hands as Ki attacked. Ki's foot smashed the agent's arms back into his face, and the wall cracked behind his head with brutal force as he bounced against it.

Ki whirled as he sensed Bolan behind him. The two men's attacks spun into each other. The entranced Javanese made no attempt to block. His foot scythed for Bolan's head. The big American held the pineapple grenade in his open right fist. His blow swung around in a brutal arc like a ball and chain. The crenellated steel sphere of the fragmentation grenade crunched into Ki's temple. Ki's kick struck Bolan's blocking arm a split second later and staggered him halfway across the room.

Bolan kept his feet. He steadied himself and staggered back to the fray with the bloody grenade in his hand.

The soldier brought the grenade up overhead and smashed it into the crown of Ki's skull. Ki fell on his face. Bolan put the grenade back in his pocket and bent woodenly to retrieve his Beretta. He ejected the nearly spent clip and reloaded. "Poulain? You all right?"

Poulain groaned from where he lay on the floor. The left side of his face was grotesquely swollen. *"Oui..."* He nodded and even that effort seemed to hurt him. The doctor looked about painfully for his rifle.

"Roland?"

Aretos sat collapsed against the wall. Blood poured down the back of his head. His left forearm was broken in two places. The blackening bruises on his throat reduced his voice to a guttural whisper. He cursed in French.

Bolan smiled tiredly. If the Frenchman could use foul language, he could breathe. The soldier picked up his fallen Thompson. He clicked in his last 50-round drum and racked the action. "Roland, you and Poulain hold the fort up here. I'm going down." Bolan picked up his Beretta and held it out. "If anyone besides me or Jolie comes up the stairs, shoot them."

Aretos nodded and grimaced as he took the pistol in his good hand.

Bolan nodded at Poulain. "Watch the door."

Poulain sat wearily next to Aretos and aimed his rifle. Bolan picked his way over the bodies of the two dead gangsters on the stair. Reno lay at the foot of the stairwell. Ki's shotgun blast had decapitated him. Bolan picked up the shotgun and entered the cellar. It was a fairly spacious room. Chains and shackles were bolted to the concrete walls. A twisted, all stainless-steel version of a dentist's chair dominated the room. It had multiple restraints and could be adjusted into numerous positions. The stains on the floor and the stench of human suffering testified to what sort of things went down in the tiny concrete hell below the earth. Ugly implements of torture lay arranged on wheeled trays, as well as a pair of video cameras. There were two doors off to the side.

Jolie's torn clothes were tossed in a corner.

Bolan kicked a door and found an empty cell. He kicked the second, and Jolie Erulin lay naked upon the floor. Her nose was bleeding, and her left eye was swollen shut. Bolan knelt.

"Are you all right?"

She shuddered. "I do not wish to speak of it."

Bolan quickly checked her over. The lack of outward damage implied they had not gotten around to any of the real fun yet. She shook uncontrollably, but her good eye blazed at Bolan. "Don't let my men see me like this."

Bolan collected her garments. He pulled off his jacket and wrapped it around her shoulders as she struggled to pull on her torn clothes. Bolan handed her the fallen shotgun. "How's that?"

She clutched the shotgun. "Better." She suddenly became aware of Reno's body at the foot of the stairs. "Roland…"

"He's injured, but alive. Poulain is with him."

"Bernard?"

"He insisted on coming to rescue you."

"He is a fool," the agent murmured.

Bolan nodded. "You have that effect."

She smiled weakly.

Bolan jerked his head toward the stairs. "Let's get you out of here."

13

"Roland is busted up." Bolan rubbed his own aching arms and ribs. The bruises had turned an ugly black. He didn't want to think about his face. "Dr. Poulain has a concussion. They're keeping him under medical observation at the hospital."

"Got to take care of France's best brain." Kurtzman was clearly more concerned about Bolan. "How are you?"

"Been worse. Massive contusions, the usual. Breathing is fun." Bolan took out some medical tape and bandaging from his kit. "Tomorrow, it's going to be a barrel of laughs."

"How is Jolie?"

"I don't know. She's not talking. She went into professional mode and is busying herself with her men." Bolan frowned. "There were no signs of significant physical torture, but there are worse things you can do to a woman than jumper cables and pliers."

Kurtzman sighed. "What did you learn?"

"Not much. Ki is dead. That he was involved with Javanese gangsters in French Guiana isn't a surprise, and we didn't take any prisoners. We took casualties. As a rescue, it was success. As a hard probe, it was a failure. We didn't learn anything, and we lost another twenty-four hours. Did you come up with anything?"

"I got some of the lowdown on Dr. Mohammed-khani."

"What'd you get?"

"You were right on the money. Feresteh Moham-medkhani emigrated from Iran with her parents Jafar and Mariam Mohammedkhani to France when she was seventeen. Both of her parents were engineers, her father chemical and her mother civil. She and her parents became French citizens. France granted them dual citizenship. Iran doesn't recognize it."

"What's the status on her parents now?"

"Both are alive and solid citizens. Jafar retired from the petrochemical business and teaches at the Polytechnical School. Mariam works for the Parisian city government."

Bolan considered the coldness he'd seen in Dr. Mohammedkhani's gray eyes. "And what about their daughter?"

Kurtzman sighed in admiration. He liked a woman with a brain. "Child prodigy. It appears to be one of the reasons the Mohammedkhanis emigrated. They wanted Feresteh to have education and employment opportunities she wouldn't have access to in an Iran under the Ayatollah. She graduated at the top of her class in the last year of middle school and then enrolled in the Polytechnical School. She got her degree in Aerospace and Systems Engineering, again at the head of her class."

Bolan watched the information scroll on the computer screen. "Give me something I can use, Bear."

Kurtzman hit some keys. "Things start to get interesting. Feresteh got involved in political activity at university."

"What kind of political activity?"

"Anti-American, anti-Israeli. She spoke at rallies and was arrested twice at protests outside the U.S. Embassy, bricks in hand. She also helped organize Muslim militants, both on and off campus. The French police investigated her on a weapons charge, but it was dropped. Probably because her parents were wealthy, high profile and very useful citizens of France. But it was enough for Israeli Intelligence to keep a passive tab on her activities."

"What happened?"

"Her political activity seems to have tapered off as she went on to get her advanced degrees and specialized in rocket science. She went to work for the space program after earning her doctorate."

"Okay, so where does Israeli Intelligence come into the picture?" Bolan asked.

Kurtzman let the cat out of the bag. "They considered assassinating her."

"Really?"

"Really. The Israelis were following up on a lead they had on Iraqi Intelligence activity. That lead led to Paris. It appears Iraqi agents contacted Dr. Mohammedkhani in 1995 and again in 1997."

Bolan could see what was coming. "To help modify and upgrade their SCUD missiles."

"That's right. The first time the Israelis detected the contact, it sent up red flags. The second time, they had a team on a flight to Paris ready to go and punch her clock."

"What stopped them?"

"They believe she refused to help the Iraqis, though there seemed to be some dancing around the second time. That's when the hit men got ready to deploy. Then, the Iraqi agents left Paris, without Dr. Mohammedkhani or any significant technical advisement or information. The hit was called off."

"How does French Intelligence feel about all this?"

"There's no indication that they know."

Bolan rose. "I think I'll just have to go have a talk with her."

Kurtzman cocked his head. "Doesn't she think you're a pig?"

"I believe she considers me an ignorant, bigoted, Muslim-hating American pig," Bolan replied.

"So you should have no trouble then."

Sinnamary, French Guiana

THE ANCIENT INDIO SERVANT looked at Bolan dubiously. So did the two drooling French Mastiffs flanking him. Bolan had looked at himself in the mirror that morning. He wouldn't let anyone with a face like his through the front door, either. He looked like he'd gone fifteen rounds well out of his weight class. Bolan's mashed lips made a dreadful attempt at a smile for the little man in the white housecoat and sarong. "I'm expected."

The old Indio's almond eyes peered up at Bolan critically. "Monsieur Cooper?"

"The same."

The man turned without a word. The dogs dropped into formation as the servant led Bolan through a French colonial–style house. It had been beautifully restored and Spartanly furnished with a tasteful mix of French and Persian antiques. The late-afternoon heat was intense, but the house was perched right on the sea, and the ocean breeze stirred the long white curtains. They went out onto the veranda, and Bolan kept the surprise off of his face. The servant bowed slightly. "Mademoiselle Mohammedkhani. Your guest is arrived."

Dr. Mohammedkhani lay upon a deck chair, sunning herself. She turned large dark sunglasses to regard Bolan. She was wearing a black bikini, and her magnificent black hair cascaded past her shoulders. The tropical sun made her already olive complexion glow. She pulled down the dark glasses to reveal her startling gray eyes. "You are early."

Bolan shrugged.

"You look like shit."

He cracked a smile through his mashed lips.

"I suppose the state of your face has something do with why Dr. Poulain is in hospital with a concussion."

Bolan saw no reason to lie. "The injuries are related."

"If Dr. Poulain were not in hospital, and had he not called me personally this morning, told me what happened and asked me to cooperate with you, I would have had Luc sic the dogs on you."

Bolan nodded. "I'm glad you didn't."

Dr. Mohammedkhani sighed magnificently. "I am still not sure if this is a good idea."

Bolan nodded. "These are serious people, Dr. Mohammedkhani."

The doctor was a beautiful woman, but her face could grow cold in an instant. She took off her sunglasses and turned her icy gaze on Bolan. "So, I am a suspect?"

"My main one at the moment, at least on paper."

"On paper?"

"Well, just on raw data. You're Iranian by birth, you've been involved in radical, anti-American political movements in Paris and you've been approached at least twice by the Iraqis to assist them in upgrading their ballistic missile systems."

She stiffened.

He pressed his advantage home. "In 1997, the Israeli Mossad had a hit team on a flight to Paris to kill you."

Her face showed her alarm.

Bolan's instincts were correct. She hadn't known about her brush with death. "On paper, you've got the tools, the talent, the means and the motivation to make something unpleasant happen involving the space center. But in person…" Bolan sat down on a chair and let the sun soak into his stiffened muscles. "You don't give off the vibe."

"Well, thank you, I suppose." The scientist's face stayed hard, but her body relaxed slightly. "I will tell you something you may not know. My father fought in the Iran-Iraq war. He came back with mustard gas burns in his lungs. My two brothers did not come back at all. My father told me to tell the Iraqis to go fuck themselves, and that is what I did."

"You're a brave woman."

"Thank you." The gray eyes did not blink. "But that still begs the question, what are you doing here?"

"I'm trying to put two and two together. Something terrible is about to happen. I don't know what it is, but I have to try to stop it. I can't leave any stone unturned." Bolan switched gears. "You respect Dr. Poulain?"

"He is a genius, and he has been my biggest sponsor. What exactly did you do that put him in hospital?"

Bolan decided to breach the security of Action Direct. "Agent Erulin was kidnapped."

"Jolie?" The woman blinked. "How? Why?"

"By Muslim terrorists. Javanese, but I believe the cell operating in French Guiana goes far beyond the Javanese in South America. She was kidnapped in an attempt to take me off the investigation, and hopefully, get French Intelligence to kill me."

"How was Dr. Poulain involved?"

"I believe that both French Intelligence and the legion have been compromised here. Which means the terrorists would have ears in the local police, as well. I gambled on trusting Agents Aretos and Reno. Dr. Poulain volunteered to back me up."

"You rescued Jolie?"

"We were successful, though Dr. Poulain was injured during the rescue, as you know. So was Roland. Alain didn't make it."

"Jolie." Dr. Mohammedkhani smiled in bemusement at the name. "I suppose she was suitably grateful."

Bolan caught the vibe in her expression but ignored it.

The gray eyes grew troubled. "Who are you?"

"Someone trying to stop the massacre of innocents."

"You really believe that the space center is somehow going to be involved in a terrorist attack?"

"I know it. I know it in my bones." Bolan's lips skinned back from his teeth in frustration. "But pieces are missing, and I can't quite put the puzzle together. I'm trying to stop an atrocity, Feresteh, and I know your first instinct is to tell me to go stand in front of an Israeli tank in the West Bank, but..." Bolan relaxed and smiled again. "This isn't an interrogation. Like I told

Dr. Poulain, I was only hoping something you might suggest, or just say unknowingly, might help."

The scientist regarded Bolan intently. "But I am still your number-one suspect."

"On paper, like I said." Bolan met her look. "In person, I'm not so sure anymore."

She stood. Her glossy black hair surged forward as she threw a long leg over Bolan and straddled his stomach. "If we are going to cooperate—" she leaned down and her gray eyes bore into his "—you're going to have to be absolutely sure."

14

"Sleeping with the enemy?" Kurtzman was vaguely appalled.

"Winning friends and gaining influence," Bolan countersuggested.

"So what did you learn?"

"Not much in the way of hard data. Instinctwise, I don't think she is directly involved in any kind of terrorist plot, but that doesn't mean she isn't being used, either with or without her knowing it, or she may think she is involved in something else. Some of the things I told her shook her up. She says she wants to cooperate."

"So Ki's dead, and you've seduced every woman with a top-secret clearance in French Guiana." Kurtzman folded his arms. "Where does that leave us?"

"It leaves us with a space shot out of Kourou in four days, and I still have a really bad feeling about it."

"Question is, what do you want to do about it? The French government isn't going to stop a space launch on our say-so, particularly when we have nothing to go on but your gut feelings. They're probably already ticked off with all of our meddling."

Bolan knew he was right. With Ki dead, French Intelligence probably considered the matter closed, and even though Bolan had rescued Erulin, he had gotten one of their agents killed and risked one of France's top scientific minds. Action Direct and the French government probably didn't feel he had done them any favors. He'd exposed a mess and been a major source of embarrassment. It was only a matter of time before they had him officially booted out of French Guiana.

"This all started with the foreign legion. That's what I'm going to have to go back to. Hopefully, Jolie will have something I can use, regardless. I'm going to drop a dime on Commandant Marmion. I'll contact you when I have something."

"All right, I'll keep working it from my end."

Bolan clicked open his phone and punched the preset number. The phone answered in two rings. "Marmion."

"Good evening, Commandant. I trust your friend Captain Cunningham contacted you yesterday."

"Yes, he did. He said he does not completely understand what is going on, but that he has been assured by the highest levels of U.S. Military Intelligence that you are to be trusted, and that the security of both of our nations is at risk." The French officer's voice was cold. He was clearly not happy.

Bolan's battle instincts went on alert. "Something has happened."

"Yes, something has happened. I think you should come here, and you should speak with Ilyanov."

"I'm on my way." Bolan clicked the phone shut.

Jungle Warfare Camp

THE BIG RUSSIAN GLARED out the window of his tiny office into the inky blackness of the night. "As you know, I have been keeping track of Legionnaires Sahin and Atrache."

Bolan nodded. "The Turk and the Algerian."

Ilyanov stood like a statue. "When a man joins the legion, he is given the opportunity to change his identity."

"So I've heard."

"It is not like the old days, when rapists, murderers, or any scum with prices on their heads could take the oath and disappear. We do background checks on any applicant who is initially accepted. This check is performed by Interpol." Ilyanov shook his head slowly. "As you can imagine, many things are missed, but in some ways, we do not care. If we find no glaring fault with you, your past is your past. It is your behavior while in the legion that concerns myself and my branch of the legion the most."

"I understand."

"Nevertheless, I have dug into the past of every Muslim legionnaire in French Guiana." Ilyanov shrugged. "I myself am Jewish. I have a number of friends and relatives who have emigrated to Israel."

"You have some connections in the Mossad," Bolan concluded.

"Yes. I have called in favors, and I can tell you this. Caporal Rachid Atrache has a death sentence on his head. He has been involved with the jihad movement and the arming and equipping of terrorists in the Middle East. If Israeli Intelligence can locate him, they will attempt to kill him."

Bolan took a deep breath and let it out. "And the Turk, Sahin?"

"Caporal Lala Sahin is not a Turk. He is a Kurd. He has been involved in terrorist bombing attacks in both Turkey and Iraq for the Free Kurdistan movement. Both countries wish him dead, and he fled his homeland to Egypt and then Saudi Arabia, where it seems he sold his talents to both al Qaeda and Islamic Jihad."

Bolan could see what was coming. "And where are Atrache and Sahin now?"

"Caporals Atrache and Sahin have been listed absent without leave since 0400 hours yesterday." The brutal smile Bolan remembered returned to Ilyanov's face. "However, I think I may have an idea of where they have gone."

Bolan raised a skeptical eyebrow. "And I'm invited?"

"Commandant Marmion has ordered me to extend the offer." Ilyanov clearly wasn't pleased. "As professional courtesy."

"Where are they?"

"There is a small mosque here in Cayenne. Both men had permission to attend services there when their schedules permitted." Ilyanov pulled a map of the city from his pocket and spread it on the table. A red circle marked the mosque. "Here. According to informants, a man matching Sahin's description was seen in the vicinity of the mosque yesterday evening, in civilian clothing. Atrache has not been spotted. But if any of your suspicions have any ground, then this is where they will make contact with their confederates. One way or another."

"We stake it out?"

"We take it out." Ilyanov's expression was iron. "Sahin, Atrache and anyone who is helping them."

"How soon?"

"Now."

Bolan took a long breath. The legion took care of its own. It did not sound like Ilyanov cared about stopping terrorism. He wanted to avenge the honor of the legion, and he probably didn't care how that effected Bolan's probe. The only way Bolan could influence the outcome was to go along.

The Executioner nodded. "Let's do it."

Cayenne

"YOU HAVE weapon?"

The Executioner felt the sudden urge to lie. He had surrendered his 93-R and his knife at the gates to the camp. They had not been returned to him. But at the gate he had not turned out his pockets. He sat in the passenger seat of a civilian Peugeot. A caravan of three such vehicles wound their way through the streets of the capital. Each car was crammed with French foreign legion deep reconnaissance commandos. All of them were in civilian clothing. "No. I figured all I had was observer status."

"Use this." Ilyanov reached into a knapsack between his feet and pulled out a sound-suppressed Beretta 92-G. "You are familiar with it?"

Bolan took the pistol and checked the loads. "I'm familiar with it."

"This pistol is untraceable. If situation goes out of control, dispose of it. You will be on your own."

"I understand."

"I am in total command." Ilyanov's face went stone again. "You are here as a courtesy."

Bolan nodded. "I understand."

The car behind them peeled off down a side street as they approached the mosque. It was a small building with businesses on either side of it. It was eleven in the evening, and the businesses were all closed. There was no one on the street.

Ilyanov nodded as he listened to his phone. "Flanking team is in position." He brought the car to a halt across the street from the mosque. "Let's go."

The four of them went EVA. The four men from the other car got out, and Bolan's eyes narrowed as he saw Roland Aretos was one of them. The Action Direct agent's left arm was in a cast, and his face was still swollen. He carried a silenced Beretta low against his leg with his good hand. He seemed surprised to see Bolan, but acknowledged him with a nod.

It seemed all of France wanted payback on Atrache and Sahin this night.

The assault team crossed the street and took the steps up to the mosque. Ilyanov tried the double doors and found them locked. They smashed inward as he put his foot into the lock. They fanned out into the mosque. The high-ceilinged building was dimly lit and seemed empty. Other than some low tables, the only furniture was the elevated pulpit where sermons were delivered to the faithful.

"Lights," Ilyanov grunted.

A gigantic black legionnaire found the lights and flicked them on.

Bolan kept one hand in his pocket and his pistol trained on a door in the back of the mosque.

The Executioner turned at the sound of the doors being closed and barred behind them.

The big black legionnaire smiled.

Ilyanov grinned from ear to ear. His pistol was pointed between Bolan's eyes.

Off to the side, a pistol clicked three times in rapid succession. Aretos had his Beretta pointed at Ilyanov's head. The hammer fell twice more. The action did not cycle. No cough came from the sound suppressor. The hammer just fell, clicking emptily. Bolan didn't bother pulling the trigger on the weapon he'd been given. Every round within it was a dud.

He'd been set up.

Aretos glared at Ilyanov through the mask of bruises on his face.

"Drop the pistols," Ilyanov ordered. He smiled at Bolan infuriatingly. "And you, take your hand out of your pocket. Very slowly."

Four silenced Berettas were trained on Bolan. Aretos had three of his own to face. The dummy pistols dropped to the carpet with dull thuds. Bolan very slowly took his hand out of his pocket. He had already pulled the pin from the pineapple grenade once this day. The crimp that held it in place had been pulled straight. It slid out with a flick of his thumb as his hand came out of his jacket. The pin fell to the floor of the mosque with barely a sound as he revealed what he held.

The legionnaires stared in surprise and horror at the grenade in Bolan's hand. They were all trained soldiers. The doors were barred. There was no cover, and every man knew he was within the lethal radius of the grenade.

Aretos grinned with savage triumph at the sight of the grenade in Bolan's hand.

Ilyanov looked askance at the ugly, serrated gray lump of steel Bolan held. "You're bluffing."

Bolan's eyes were icy.

Ilyanov swallowed.

"Do it," Aretos suggested.

Ilyanov's gun never wavered. "Killing us here won't stop it."

"Stop what?" Bolan asked.

Ilyanov was silent.

"A grenade going off in a downtown mosque, killing seven out-of-uniform legionnaires and an Action Direct agent might cause a big enough stink to start a real investigation. What do you think?"

"I think it is an excellent idea." Aretos waggled his eyebrows. Action Direct really did believe in payback. Right to the very end. "Do it," the French agent repeated.

Bolan and Ilyanov stood face-to-face, unmoving. The Executioner detected something he didn't like. Ilyanov was clearly trying to figure an angle.

But the Russian was also clearly willing to die.

"Fuck this." Aretos's right hand blurred. With a snap of his wrist a switchblade came out of his sleeve. The blade clicked open as it left his fingers and scythed like a quicksilver gleam through the air at Ilyanov.

The three men covering him all shot the French agent in the chest at the same time.

The cotter pin pinged away as Bolan dropped his grenade.

Ilyanov staggered as the knife sank into his neck.

Two bullets hit Bolan in the chest, and the wind of two more hissed past his face as the giant African and another legionnaire went for head shots. Bolan staggered, but his armor held. He turned and took two bullets between the shoulder blades as he dived for the pulpit.

Behind him, the locked and barred doors to the mosque splintered as the giant legionnaire applied his bulk to them. Bolan rolled behind the ornate staircase of the pulpit as the grenade detonated with a crack.

Men screamed as shreds of jagged metal buzz-sawed through the mosque in all directions. The pulpit rattled as it was scored with shrapnel. Bolan was up instantly. Four legionnaires and Aretos were down. The doors to the mosque were flung open. The soldier dived for two of the fallen legionnaires. One was motionless, and one moaned. Both had been torn bloody by the fragmentation grenade. Bolan ripped the silenced Berettas from their hands.

"Hey…" Aretos groaned weakly.

Bolan kept both pistols trained on the door as he visually examined the Frenchman. His clothes were torn, but his torso was conspicuously free of blood. His arms and legs were another matter. No soft body armor covered his limbs, and he was bleeding like a stuck pig. His face was badly torn and one of his eyes was pulp in its socket.

"You…have another grenade?" he asked Bolan.

"Yeah."

"Give it to me…I'll let go of it when they rush us. You…shoot from cover."

"No." Bolan shook his head. He didn't like the Frenchman at all, but he had to admit Aretos was as hard-core as they came. "We're going out the back."

Bolan grunted with the agent's weight as he put him over his shoulder in a fireman's carry. He put one of the pistols in his hand. "Shoot, if you can."

The soldier took his second grenade and pulled the pin. He moved to the back of the mosque, keeping himself out of line of sight with the front doors. As Bolan approached the back, he could hear people moving in the back room. Bolan kicked the door and rolled the grenade into the room. Shouts of alarm sounded in several languages, but Bolan had already stepped behind the jamb. The grenade detonated, and Bolan staggered in, bearing Aretos like a sack of potatoes. A legionnaire howled, clutching his face. Another lay still with hardly any face left to clutch. Both men were riddled with metal fragments. The room had a wall for hanging jackets and a small kitchen. The back door flung open, and a legionnaire hurtled inside demanding to know what was happening. He only had time to widen his eyes as Bolan shot him twice in the chest. Concealable soft body armor was not legion issue.

Bolan stepped outside. He grunted under Aretos as a bullet hit him in the stomach. The soldier took another hit as he brought his pistol to bear on the legionnaire by the idling car. His first shot spiderwebbed the windshield. Aretos wheezed as he took a bullet in his side meant for Bolan's head. The Executioner awkwardly adjusted his aim. Bolan's first shot shattered the man's clavicle. His second tore out the legionnaire's throat.

Bolan tottered down the tiny flight of steps to the street and piled Aretos into the back of the car. He slid behind the wheel. Three men came around the corner. Ilyanov stood with the knife still in his neck. The African and a smaller man stood with him. All three began emptying their pistols at the car.

The Executioner rammed the car into gear and aimed straight for Ilyanov. The huge African yanked the Russian to one side even as he kept shooting. The windshield pocked and cracked with bullet strikes. Bolan jerked his head below the dash, and the headrest tore with bullet strikes as glass rained down. He swerved the car but was not rewarded with the thump of a body. Bolan swung the car back as bullets began hitting the rear windshield. He rose up and yanked the wheel. His rear tire spit off its hubcap as it turned the corner with a scream.

"Did we get him?" Aretos asked.

Bolan took the car back out onto the street. He drove past the two parked cars and put a bullet into each tire facing the street. "You got a piece of him."

"I must…check in."

"You need to check into a hospital."

"Unnh." Aretos wheezed noncommittally. "And you?"

Bolan grimaced at his pulverized rib cage. No one in the legion could be trusted. Someone had been willing to sacrifice Aretos. His car was shot up, and he could not afford to be stopped by the police.

"I don't know. Maybe I'll lay low. Go get laid."

The Frenchman's laugh was a bubbling wheeze. "Good…good for you."

BABAR TOOK the knife in his hand and put his other massive mitt on the Commander's shoulder. Ilyanov didn't flinch as Babar pulled the blade free. It had just missed his carotid artery. Cigarette reloaded his Beretta and went into the mosque. They had minutes before the city police began arriving.

Babar wiped the bloody knife on his pant leg and closed it. The Commander already had his handkerchief pressed against the wound.

"What do we do, Commander?"

"Contingencies were planned for. Now we must do damage control. His access to the Jungle Warfare camp must be cut off. All of his intelligence assets in French Guiana must be cut off."

"And?"

Ilyanov looked into the future. "And he only has seventy-two hours left."

15

Sinnamary

Jolie Erulin's voice was tightly controlled over the phone. "Where are you?"

Bolan stood at the edge of the water as the morning tide rolled in. "Someplace safe, for the moment. How is Roland?"

"He is stable." Her voice relented somewhat. "I must thank you. He says you saved his life…after you blew him up."

"He told me to go ahead and do it." Bolan considered the brutal Frenchman. "He's tough, I'll give him that."

"I do not love him, personally, but he is our best in South America, or was. He will be relegated to a desk now, if he does not retire." Her voice hardened again. "Where are you? You should not have gone to the mosque without telling me. That was foolish."

"I went to rescue you from Ki without telling the foreign legion. That was probably for the best."

She accepted that with silence.

"Sorry, but even if I'd wanted to, I wasn't given the

opportunity." Bolan's voice hardened to match the French agent's silence. "Where's Ilyanov, and who is he?"

Agent Erulin paused for a long moment. Bolan almost thought she had hung up before she finally spoke.

"Due to recent activity, Action Direct has broken into the foreign legion database. If this gets back to French Military Intelligence, there will be—"

"Lady, I don't have time for political considerations, and neither do you. Spill it."

"We ignored the Interpol background checks and used our own files. Then we called in favors with British and U.S. Intelligence."

"What did you find?"

"Ilyanov changed his name when he joined the legion. This is not unusual, over half the legion is from Russia and the former Eastern Bloc, and apply simply as Slavs. They—"

"Short version," Bolan said impatiently.

"His real name is Valentjin Islamov. He was a rebel in Muslim Chechnya. When his activities began to include bombings in Moscow, he was forced to flee. He spent time in the Middle East before joining the legion."

"There was an African with him at the mosque, huge. What's his story?"

"Babacar 'Babar' N'Dour, Senegalese. Former heroin dealer until his conversion to Islam. He is Islamov's adjutant in the Jungle Warfare School."

Bolan saw an ugly trend. "And both men are involved in security at the launch facility."

"Yes, as is Truong Nguyen Ngoc, 'Knock-Knock' as he is called. A Vietnamese Muslim. Engaged in terrorist activity in Indonesia and wanted by the Australians for the murder of UN peacekeepers in Timor. Sretko "Cigarette" Tadic claimed to be a Serb when he joined the legion, but he is a Bosnian Muslim. Atrache and Sahin you already knew about. The rest of the men you killed in the mosque are unimportant, for the moment, but have similar backgrounds. What is more important, is that all the men I have mentioned are now AWOL from the Jungle Warfare camp."

Bolan's world got uglier by the second. "What about Marmion? He's their commanding officer. Have you investigated him?"

"Commandant Marmion is dead."

Bolan was shocked. "How?"

"He was found in his office last night. About an hour after the battle at the mosque. He was bleeding from the ears and the tear ducts." Erulin paused. "Closer examination reveled a .32-caliber exploding bullet was introduced into his brain through the back of his head."

Bolan grimaced. Another good man had gone down. "What did you find out at the space port?"

"Is Dr. Mohammedkhani with you?"

Bolan turned back to his little camp. He had come back to Sinnamary half expecting to find her kidnapped or dead. He had put her on the back of his bike with a sleeping bag, and they had driven up to the coast to an abandoned bit of beach. Bolan had grabbed a few desperately needed hours of sleep. The scientist lay in the bag, her head veiled by the masses of her dark hair. "Yeah, she's with me."

"You are at her house?"

"No, but she's out of earshot at the moment."

"Good."

Bolan heard the urgency in Erulin's voice. "What is it?"

"I spoke with Dr. Seth last night. Babu Seth. You met him in the space center lounge."

"I remember him. The payload engineer."

"Yes. You kept thinking that somehow the launch was going to be involved in some sort of terrorist atrocity. I spent a number of hours last night consulting with him, to see if we could find any kind of discrepancy, and—"

"And you found one."

"Dr. Seth is thorough. He checked everything, and then he checked his own records. He found that industrial quality powdered cobalt had been purchased and shipped to the space center satellite division, under his name, and using his security codes."

Bolan's blood went cold. "I gather Dr. Seth does not recall buying any cobalt?"

"No, much less two thousand kilograms of it."

"Where is the cobalt now?"

"That is just it. It is not in the warehouse where it is supposed to be. We tracked the transaction to a South African firm. The South African distributor assures us that the metal was paid for, shipped and sent. All perfectly legal. Action Direct is checking all stages of the transaction, but so far it seems like the distributor is telling the truth. We are acting on the assumption that the cobalt disappeared on the South American end of the deal."

"You believe Feresteh bought the cobalt using Dr. Seth's clearance and identification codes."

"Cobalt is a metal used extensively in modern manufacturing. There is nothing suspicious about it, alone. The space center manufacturing division here in French Guiana goes through tons of it every year. The only discrepancy is that two thousand kilograms were bought under false pretenses. If Dr. Seth had not stayed up until four in the morning personally checking inventories, it could have gone unnoticed for the rest of the year."

"You think Feresteh did it."

"The only other likely suspects are Dr. Dutronc and Dr. Poulain. Both of them are native Frenchmen, both with unimpeachable security records. Dr. Seth is a Hindu, and very unlikely to be lying, much less cooperating with Muslim extremists."

"Feresteh doesn't give off the vibe."

Erulin's voice grew nasty. "I am sure Dr. Mohammedkhani gave you a good vibe in bed. But it is you who are running around French Guiana claiming terrorist plots of massive proportions. You and I both know that the only use a terrorist has for cobalt is to sheath it around a nuclear weapon to make a dirty bomb. She has the background, she had the means, she has the talent, and given her past, I am assuming she has the motivation. Two thousand kilograms of cobalt were acquired illegally, and now they are missing."

Bolan accepted every word Erulin said, but his instincts told him she was wrong. "Something's missing."

"Can't you Americans ever accept the fact that you might be wrong!" Erulin erupted. "What if I told you that last year Dr. Mohammedkhani became a fully licensed multiengine pilot, and is currently working on her helicopter qualification?"

"It would make her a very able woman."

"Yes, but what if I also told you she is a member of the Kourou Shooting Club, and owns a .32-caliber Unique target pistol?"

Bolan's stomach tightened.

"And what if I told you that after this weekend's launch she is scheduled to fly to the United States to an aerospace conference in Washington, D.C.?"

Bolan turned back to look at the sleeping figure between the dunes.

"The President of France will be there for his own meeting with your President."

Bolan's hand went to his pistol. The rocket scientist would not have to ram her plane into the White House. She would not even have to get particularly near it. All that would be required would be to get airborne over the D.C. area in a plane and detonate a weapon. Sheathed in cobalt, even a tactical nuke would kill most everyone in the capital in gruesome fashion.

Erulin's voice went dead. "Dr. Mohammedkhani is coming in. Dead or alive, but she is not getting on a plane to the U.S. I am letting you know out of professional courtesy, and personally, I advise you to leave French Guiana. There is talk in my department of bringing you in and having you…interrogated. I appreciate your efforts, and that you saved my life, but I am only field coordinator, and you have pissed off all the wrong people above my pay class."

Bolan's eyes never left the sleeping woman. "You're not telling me everything."

"We have gone over deployment schedules in the Jungle Warfare camp. Particularly training missions led by Babacar. Almost all of them were teams made up of the Muslim legionnaires. We believe they have set up a base in the jungle. We have photographed it by satellite."

"Take me there."

"That would be highly irregular. The Jungle Warfare Camp is in lockdown status." Her voice grew bitter. "I have been ordered to stand down and wait for the strike team to be sent from Paris. They will be here in four hours."

"Tell your superiors you went to meet me. Tell them you did it under pretense to bring me in. Then we go on a detour. After that, I'll be happy to debrief your superiors on everything we have on our side."

Erulin was silent as she slowly overcame her better judgment. "Tell me where Dr. Mohammedkhani is. I will dispatch people to pick her up. She will only be held. I will work with you for the remaining hours on your hunch. That is the best I can do. Then it will be beyond my hands"

"Done."

"Meet me at the space center." Erulin's voice brightened slightly. "I have a helicopter there."

THE JUNGLE FLEW BY in a solid green carpet beneath the Dauphin helicopter. The aircraft roared barely inches above the jungle canopy. Flights of multicolored birds burst from the treetops, and bats blasted upward in flapping black clouds in the helicopter's wake. Bolan had left Mohammedkhani back at her house and the chopper had been hot on the pad and Erulin waiting for him at the space center when he arrived. Erulin's gaze flicked down to her instruments. "We should be getting close." She followed the path a river cut through the rain forest.

"How far are we from the Jungle Warfare camp?"

"About a hundred kilometers. We are in the center of French Guiana. There is nothing out here but jungle.

Even the Indians do not come here. There is nothing but snakes and spiders, leopards, piranha, leeches and crocodiles here." Her shoulders twitched. "Only legionnaires would come to a place like this."

Bolan pointed. "There."

A finger of creek broke off from the river and traced a path through the jungle. It opened out into a pond and a small clearing and disappeared again. At the edges of the clearing, the trees were strung with camouflage netting. Erulin slowly orbited the camp and then broke off and did a larger orbit around the jungle surrounding it.

Bolan shook his head. There could be an entire regiment of foreign legion deep reconnaissance commandos pointing their rifles at them and they'd never know it.

Erulin seemed to read his mind. "You are the one who did not wish to wait for the strike team." She brought the helicopter back to the clearing. The Dauphin's landing gear slid out and Erulin set her down.

Bolan slid out of the helicopter. He had not had time to pick up a full warload. Nor was he going to trust any gun he hadn't personally fired. The ancient Thompson was cradled in his hands with a 50-round drum in place. He carried both of the silenced Berettas he'd taken from the mosque. His pockets were full of grenades.

Erulin jumped out of the pilot's seat and scooped up a FAMAS assault rifle. Bolan scanned the area. He had seen a million such camps before. There was a clearing suitable for a single helicopter, a water source, and a few benches and tables hewn out of logs beneath the cover of the trees. It was a typical rest and resupply area for troops on maneuvers in friendly territory. The threshing of the rotor blades and the leaves and dirt it kicked up ruined any opportunity to pick up on sound or movement. Bolan glanced at the ground. There were many boot prints in the soft earth. All of their treads matched the legionnaire pattern he had observed in Suriname. Most of the tracks looked several days old.

Bolan moved beneath the trees.

It took only moments to find the bunker.

Earth had been mounded over the sunken log construction so that it looked like little more than a rise in the soil of the jungle. A very wide double door of heavy, unfinished beams formed the entrance. The ground in front of it had been rolled flat by something very heavy. The Thompson hammered the padlock from the oversize door with a single burst. There were no steps, but a shallow ramp ran down into the darkness. A ramp wide enough to accommodate heavy pallets. There was a generator, but Bolan did not turn it on. He took out his flashlight as he entered and played it over the interior. The bunker was a single low, wide room. The floor was packed earth, the walls were held in place by planking and the ceilings by beams of tree trunk hewn directly from the surrounding forest.

It was job a squad of men could easily have done with hand tools over the course of several "training deployments." There were crates and boxes toward the back. Erulin descended the ramp, shining her own flashlight around the bunker. Bolan found a rifle crate for six weapons. Three rifles were gone. Three FAMAS assault rifles were still packaged. Several thousand rounds of .223-caliber ammunition were stacked next to the rifles in canisters, some of them opened. Bolan found a suitcase filled with euros. A pair of French Mistral man-portable, surface-to-air-missile systems stood in the corner. Their tripods and optical units were in place. Both launch tubes had a missile loaded and ready to go. "We were lucky no one was here to meet us," he said.

"I do not think our presence here matters anymore." Erulin knelt in an empty corner. She traced her fingers through the dirt.

Bolan came over and found the dirt was compacted and marked over a broad, six-foot by four-foot area, as if it had borne a very heavy weight. Bolan squatted and took a bit of the dirt between his fingers. The soil of the bunker was dark and slightly moist. Bolan shone his flashlight over his fingers. Intermixed with the dark dirt were flecks of bright blue.

Cobalt-blue.

The cobalt was no longer simply missing. It had been deployed.

Bolan rose. "I have to contact my people."

He stopped as he heard the sound of a FAMAS rifle selector switch flicking to full-auto behind him. Bolan stood still for a moment. The .45-caliber slugs in his submachine gun would not pierce her soft body armor. His own armor was not rated against a .223-caliber rifle bullet on its best days, and his armor had taken a severe beating over the past seventy-two hours.

Erulin spoke very quietly. "I have orders to take you in for interrogation."

Bolan slowly turned. He kept his muzzle pointed toward the floor even as he gauged the head shot. "I'm not going."

Conflicting emotions played across the woman's face. She sighed bitterly as she lowered the muzzle of her rifle. "I know. Take the helicopter. I will call for extraction. I will tell them…" She looked away. "I will tell them you overpowered me."

Bolan nodded and left the bunker. He climbed behind the stick of the Dauphin and powered up her engines. The rotors beat the sky and the chopper lifted off the ground. As he brought the nose of the helicopter around, his eyes flew wide.

Valentjin Islamov stood next to Erulin. Beside him, Babacar had set down the firing tripod of a Mistral missile system and slid into the chair. Islamov waved cheerily.

Bolan rammed the throttles forward into emergency power.

Erulin pursed her perfect lips against her fingers and blew Bolan a kiss goodbye.

The helicopter's twin engines roared over the soldier's head as the rotors clawed for altitude. Treetops scraped the bottom of the fuselage and dipped the Dauphin's nose. Bolan banked desperately. The helicopter swooped forward but not fast enough. He threw a glance backward. A smear of yellow fire trailing black smoke flew after him just above the trees. It was moving at sickening speed.

The Dauphin was a commercial aircraft. It had no infrared flares or countermeasures. The Executioner rammed the stick to the right and the landing gear ripped through the treetops as the chopper banked radically. Bolan kept the throttles full, but the Dauphin was already giving him everything she had. If the missile had locked, the only advantage he had was that the range was point-blank and his helicopter could turn much harder than the missile as it accelerated to Mach 3.

Bolan yanked his stick to the left and turned into the missile's path and tried to outturn it. The Dauphin screamed as it redlined beyond tolerance into a turn it had not been designed for. Bolan gritted his teeth as—

The helicopter spun 360 degrees in the air as something struck it. The airframe shuddered as three kilograms of high explosive embedded with hundreds of tungsten steel balls ripped through the tail boom like shredding paper. Red lights lit up across the instrument board. Smoke poured out of the vents. Bolan did not have to look back to know he no longer had a tail rotor.

The helicopter was completely out of control.

Dr. Mohammedkhani was not going to be terminated, nor even arrested. She would unknowingly do her job and make sure the upcoming launch went off perfectly. Dr. Seth was the enemy. Bolan suspected he was not the Hindu he pretended to be. Kurtzman was right. There had been no modifications to the rocket or any special reentry vehicle built. The weapon was the satellite itself, built by Dr. Seth's team. It would fall, with much less accuracy than a guided rocket; but even if it missed Washington, D.C., completely, some part of the U.S. Eastern Seaboard would be turned into a radioactive wasteland.

Bolan knew that he himself was about to officially die in a tragic helicopter accident while working in cooperation with Action Direct.

Nothing was going to interfere with the upcoming launch.

These thoughts burned across Bolan's mind in the half second it took the Dauphin's composite rotor blades to snap off against the treetops. The tailless, rotorless burning airframe plowed down through canopy trailing fire into the jungle below.

16

The camouflaged men appeared out of the rain forest like phantoms. They were armed to the teeth. The man with the sniper rifle hung back and scanned the surroundings with his optical sight. Two men with rifle grenades fixed to the muzzles of their weapons fanned out to put the area in crossfire.

Islamov, Babar and Knock-Knock approached the burning wreck of the helicopter in a widely spaced crescent formation. Javanese gunmen flared out behind them.

The Dauphin was burned out, blackened and still oozing smoke.

"Babar." Islamov jerked his chin forward. "Knock-Knock."

The two legionnaires circled the hulk from opposite sides. Both men began poking in the wreckage with their bayonets. The Vietnamese quickly held up a Beretta, its grips melted by heat. Babar fished out a Thompson submachine gun with a shattered stock. The huge African straightened as he made out the blackened lump of a grenade that hadn't cooked off under one of the crumpled seats. He made rapid gestures at Knock-Knock, and the two men backed away from the crash.

Islamov spoke. "And?"

"There is no body, Commander." Babar looked around. "Though I fail to see how a man could live through such a crash." He shrugged. "The windows are shattered. Perhaps he was thrown clear."

"He is not dead until we find his body."

Babar examined the impenetrable canopy above. The helicopter had ripped a swath down to the jungle floor, but bats, eagles and monkeys could be feasting on the American's broken body, hung up on any one of the arboreal tiers, and they would never know it. "We did not bring climbing spikes, Commander."

Knock-Knock was kneeling a few feet from the wreckage. "We will not need them."

Islamov stalked forward. "What have you found?"

Knock-Knock held up his hand. There were thin streaks of red on it. "Blood." He pointed into the trees. "He went that way."

Babar stared into the dense jungle. "He is without food or water and a hundred kilometers from the camp. He is hurt. Perhaps we should let the jungle kill him rather than risk the men."

Islamov nodded and jerked his head where Knock-Knock had pointed. "Fan out. Find him. Assume he is armed."

BOLAN WAS HURT. He wasn't sure how badly, but the situation was bad enough. His side was torn. Only his body armor had prevented him from being disembow-eled. He was bleeding, and his stomach and chest radiated bands of pain that made it hard to breathe. His left eye was closed. The right eye was going in and out of focus. The blood pouring into it wasn't helping. The last two fingers of his left hand were broken. He checked the loads of the Beretta he'd managed to keep hold of during the crash. There were fifteen rounds in the magazine plus one in the chamber

He had a hand grenade.

He needed a rifle.

He also needed food, water and medical attention. Bolan checked his watch. He needed to get to the space center in Kourou within the next sixty hours, or barring that, to find a phone. The Jungle Warfare camp was sixty-two miles away through trackless jungle. He had a vague idea that there was a town twenty-five or thirty miles west, but his mental map of inland French Guiana was vague, at best. Bolan licked his split lips. He was already parched.

The Executioner tore strips from the hem of his shirt and tied his broken fingers together.

He watched from cover as the legionnaires began to follow his trail. He eyed the FRF-1 sniper rifle with a marksman's hunger. The legionnaires were fanning out, and already they were predicting his course. Most fools would have run. Islamov wasn't stupid enough to think Bolan a fool. They would be expecting him to double back toward the temporary camp where there were weapons and supplies. Bolan began ghosting the legionnaires. He'd had little time since the crash. The legionnaires swiftly came to the place where he had started trying to cover his tracks. They knew Bolan had some French, so they used Arabic as their battle language to deny Bolan intelligence. There were eighteen opponents. He figured at least half of them were Javanese in legion uniform.

Bolan pulled the pin from his remaining grenade.

Knock-Knock knelt where Bolan's blood trail stopped. He gauged the ground ahead trying to pick up the trail again. Knock-Knock suddenly looked back in alarm.

Bolan lobbed his grenade.

Knock-Knock lost his Arabic as the dark object sailed overhead through the trees. "Grenade!"

Men dived for cover among the tree trunks. Bolan leaped on top of one of the Javanese. The man grunted as the Executioner's knee drove into his back. The grenade detonated with a whip-crack. Bats and birds exploded shrieking and cawing from the trees. Monkeys screamed in fear and outrage at the alien sound. A human screamed in agony, and others shouted back and forth in Arabic, Javanese and French. Automatic rifles sent lead spraying in all directions. Bolan's sound suppressed Beretta coughed twice. The man beneath him went limp. Bolan cut the straps of the man's knapsack and web gear and grabbed his rifle.

Islamov shouted to his men to cease-fire. The Javanese auxiliaries did not have legion discipline, and they continued to fire off long bursts at shadows beneath the trees. Bolan was less than a shadow as he crawled backward using a fallen a log for cover. Bullets cracked in supersonic flight inches over his head and ripped through the foliage. The enemy was not firing for effect, they were firing in panic. Islamov was roaring in French and Arabic at the top of his lungs.

Bolan pulled the big fade back into the jungle with his prizes.

"HE HAS A RIFLE." Babar stood over the Javanese soldier's body and shook his head. "He has rifle grenades."

Cigarette nodded unhappily. "He has food and water."

Another of the Javanese stood with a pistol in his hand. His arm and shoulder were in a sling, badly torn from grenade fragments. He glared down at the body. "He has killed my brother."

Islamov fingered his rifle. Another Javanese lay dead a few feet away. Those he could buy by the bushel. But Rachid Atrache lay dead next to him. Shrapnel had ripped out his throat and eyes. Foreign legion deep reconnaissance commandos were not so easily replaced.

No one had laid eyes on the American, and he was already down three men.

Islamov calculated the situation and thought about what he would do in the same situation. "I believe our friend's best option will be to kill all of us as quickly as possible before he succumbs to exhaustion."

Neither the legionnaires nor the Javanese were particularly pleased with the announcement.

"Don't you see? He will stalk us like a ghost. Even now he has retreated to his next ambush point. What he must do is kill all of us, or just enough of us so that he can take one of our radios and send out a message. That is his mission. His ultimate survival will be secondary to making contact with the outside and stopping the launch."

Cigarette cradled his sniper rifle uncertainly. "And so?"

"And so we deny him this option. Our survival is secondary to that." Islamov opened his hand. "Radios. Everyone." He pointed at the ground in front of him. "Here. Quickly."

Knock-Knock and Cigarette took off their tactical radios and dropped them at Islamov's feet. Islamov took out his own broadband radio and cell phone and dropped them. "Babar?"

Babar shrugged and dropped his radio and cell phone, as well. The Javanese had not been issued radios. They were assigned as two-man teams to each legionnaire. Cigarette gathered up Atrache's radio and phone and dropped them in, as well. Islamov smiled at the pile of communications gear on the jungle floor. He took out his pistol and flicked off the safety.

"Hey, asshole!" Islamov's voice boomed through the jungle in English. "Do you know what this sound is?"

The pistol barked in his hand and a tactical radio jumped and shattered apart against the toes of his boots.

"That's a dead radio!" The pistol cracked seven more times in rapid succession. Bits of plastic flew and battery packs burst apart. Islamov flicked the safety back on his pistol and holstered it.

Islamov threw back his head. "It is just us, *mon ami!* Just us and the jungle! The way it should be!" He glanced at his watch. His smile became hideous as he called out again. "Fifty-nine hours until the launch, my friend! And one hundred kilometers between you and the Jungle Warfare camp! You had better start running!"

BOLAN BOUND his side. The legion knapsack contained a medical kit with field dressings. The wound was deep and wide, and would require dozens of stitches. Bolan had used half the tube of disinfectant and bound it tightly but he had no illusions. In the jungles of French Guiana the wound would go septic within hours. He winced as he pulled the shredded remnants of his body armor back over his torso and smoothed the Velcro tabs shut. His stomach growled. Bolan took hunger as a good sign that he wasn't bleeding internally. He ripped open the stolen ration pack. His hands shook as he tore into the food.

The soldier took long swallows from the canteen until he was no longer thirsty.

Water was a concern. Bolan did not doubt that Islamov had destroyed the radios his team carried. He suspected Islamov had another radio somewhere. He would have to capture the Russian to get that information out of him. Bolan wasn't counting on that opportunity coming along any time soon. He sloshed his canteen. There was about a third left. Water was the key.

He had to get to the river.

Knock-Knock was turning out to be superlative jungle tracker. He followed Bolan's trail despite his best efforts at concealing it. The Vietnamese seemed to have an almost telepathic ability to read Bolan's trail and then examine the ground ahead to predict which way he would go. Bolan had been forced to choose random paths through the jungle rather than the smartest to try to throw off Knock-Knock. The sprint-and-sneak routine was quickly sapping his strength.

Only the fear of ambush slowed the legionnaires, and their skirmish line inexorably drove Bolan before it and away from the river. He needed to make a hole in that line and slip through it. Bolan considered one of the four rifle grenades in the legion pack. It would definitely make a hole, but the moment he fired he would announce his position to the entire hunting party, and the salvo of grenades that would come hurtling back in answer would be the end of the show.

Bolan could hear the enemy coming closer. He dearly wanted to stop Knock-Knock. He wanted Cigarette's sniper rifle even more. With that in his hands, he could start forcing the issue. But to get close enough to take either one of them in this jungle would mean getting within spitting distance of the entire squad.

Islamov was begging him to try it.

The cat-and-mouse game would just have to go on a little longer.

Bolan glanced at his empty ration tin and his field-dressing wrapper. He drew the FAMAS assault weapon's bayonet and began prying at the safety ring of one of the rifle grenades.

KNOCK-KNOCK FROZE.

He raised his fist and the skirmish line halted. Sahin knelt a few feet away. The wiry Turk had his bayonet out. He carefully thrust it beneath some leaves and came up with the green plastic wrapper of a field dressing. The Javanese next to him pointed excitedly and thrust his own bayonet into a shrub.

Sahin's voice rose to a shout. "No!"

The Javanese froze. He held an empty ration tin on the end of the bayonet. Bits of leaf and dirt fell away from it. A sliver of vine fiber that stretched back to the shrub pulled away as he dropped the tin.

In the split second delay, Knock-Knock clearly heard the flat click of the tripped contact fuse.

Yellow fire puffed around the Javanese with a crack, and he shuddered as he took the full fragmentation effect at point-blank range. Sahin fell back twisting and kicking and clutching his face.

Knock-Knock dropped flat as the unmistakable

thump of a rifle-grenade launch sounded in the jungle ahead. The grenade detonated and more screams filled the jungle. Cigarette sagged back against a tree, his face and chest covered with blood. His sniper rifle sagged in his hands.

A filthy, bloodstained ghost emerged from the jungle. The FAMAS rifle the ghost held snarled into life. Cigarette jerked and flapped against the tree as the burst tore through his chest.

The ghost ran past the Bosnian sniper and ripped his weapon out of his hands without stopping. Knock-Knock rose to one knee and leveled his rifle, but the ghost had already disappeared in the trees. Knock-Knock roared with rage. He burned a magazine into the waving undergrowth the ghost had left in its wake. Two of the Javanese fired rifle grenades, and yellow fire lit the jungle ahead. Knock-Knock burst into a run. The two Javanese leaped up and followed him. He ran a few dozen meters into the jungle and stopped. His knuckles whitened around the grip and forestock of his rifle.

The blast and fragmentation of the grenades had ripped the under brush and torn the leaf duff covering the jungle floor.

Knock-Knock smothered his rage as he got down on his hands and knees and began crawling in an ever-widening circle around the grenade effects to the find where the trail of the American resumed.

Islamov trotted up and waved him away from his tracking. "Forget it. We know he is heading for the river. We beat him there, and then let him come to us."

EXHAUSTION FORCED Bolan to stop. Cramps walked up and down his ribs, and he continued to reopen his wound. The legionnaires had passed him unknowingly in their sprint for the river, but obviously they did not care. He was in a legion jungle warfare training area. His opponents knew the lay of the land. All they had to do was head him off. The clock was ticking, and it was a countdown.

Bolan drank the last of his water and examined his prize.

Grenade shrapnel scored the FR-F1 rifle, but the telescopic sight appeared to be intact. He had ten rounds in the magazine plus one in the chamber. Bolan locked a rifle grenade onto the launching ring of his FAMAS and slung it. He hefted the FR-F1 and started walking.

It was time to go force the issue.

The legionnaires had made no effort to conceal their trail as they had passed him. Bolan followed the boot prints on the jungle floor. He walked a few hundred yards and stopped. He lay down in the dirt and clicked out the rifle's bipod. He peered through the scope with his good eye. The massive hardwoods of the rain forest formed a cathedral ahead.

It was a natural fire lane.

He could hear the river somewhere ahead.

Bolan unslung his assault rifle and clicked out its bipod. He placed the rifle in a bush facing the lane of trees and began unwrapping his remaining field dressing. After carefully tying one end of the bandage around the assault rifle's trigger, he crept a few yards off to one side and put some of the bandage's slack around a sapling. He reeled out the gauze until he could drop behind a fallen tree to put cover between himself and his weapon. Bolan hunkered down with his sniper rifle and opened its bipod. He eased himself into his firing position and began to take up slack on the bandage. The Executioner pulled until it was taut. He peered above the rim of his telescopic sight.

Bolan yanked the dressing.

On the other side of the fallen tree the rifle grenade boomed off its launcher and sailed through the cathedral of trees. Before the grenade detonated, automatic rifles ripped into response. Swarms of bullets chewed the underbrush around the abandoned rifle. Bolan put the crosshairs of his sight onto the stuttering yellow flame of muzzle-blast and fired. The sniper rifle went silent as Bolan flicked the bolt and chambered a fresh round. He yanked the dressing again and the FAMAS snarled off a short burst.

Fire poured into the position. Bolan flinched as rifle grenades detonated only a few feet away and the fallen log he was using for cover was stripped and shuddered by shell fragments. Tracers drew smoking lines through the trees.

Bolan chose the muzzle-blast of another enemy rifleman and fired. A Javanese rose, shouting and pointing at Bolan's hide. Dust flew from the front of his camouflage shirt as Bolan put a bullet into his chest. An answering burst shot over Bolan's head. The Executioner could see the man's head and shoulders through the shaking bushes as he fired. The FR-F1 bucked against Bolan's shoulder, and his opponent sagged on top of his weapon.

Bolan flicked his bolt again but crawled quickly back through the underbrush as bullets began streaming into his true position. He got behind a rock and reeled in the FAMAS rifle by the field dressing. He grabbed it by the carrying handle and ran. His heels hammered into the dirt without grace or skill as he willfully stretched out his leaden limbs for speed. He ran backward and began making a long arc through the jungle.

Bolan ran for the river.

ISLAMOV WAS DOWN to six men, including himself.

The Javanese had been fanatical and dedicated volunteers to the cause. They were suicide troopers, ready to martyr themselves without a second thought. This did not make them particularly good soldiers, much less jungle stalkers.

There were only three of them left.

Within seconds of the cease-fire, Islamov's instincts told him the American was long out of rifle shot and on the move. The American would be out of water, running out of grenades and ammunition. He was likely running out of blood and stamina, as well. He still had a vast distance to cross.

He was running out of time.

Islamov rose from his hide. "Babar."

The giant Senegalese seemed to magically grow up out of his concealment like a dark tree. "Yes, Commander."

"He is running now. He is going wide, flanking us, flat out for the river."

"Yes." The big man's voice was an angry rumble. He smiled as he read Islamov's mind. "But I do not think he can outrun me."

Islamov nodded. "Take the remaining Javanese. Go. Run him down."

Babar exposed his teeth. "You and Knock-Knock will be waiting for him at the river shore?"

"We will be waiting for you, Babar." Islamov smiled in kind. "Bring us this American's head."

Babar slapped his sheathed machete and smiled. He shucked his pack and gestured at the remaining Javanese. They shucked their packs as Babar broke into a run.

Islamov drank from his canteen and watched Babar plunge into the jungle. The Javanese were already struggling just to keep him in sight.

The giant African's stride was a thing of terrifying beauty.

Islamov jerked his head at Knock-Knock and the two deep reconnaissance commandos faded back toward the river.

THE EXECUTIONER skidded to a halt and put his back to a tree.

He could hear his opponents crashing through the underbrush behind him. They had swiftly found his trail.

Bolan had made no attempt to conceal his headlong flight, and they had made no attempt to conceal their pursuit. The only thing they weren't doing was baying like hounds. If they were smart, they would have a flanking team down by the river by now. Bolan raised the FAMAS rifle, clicked his last rifle grenade over the muzzle and stepped out from behind the tree.

The men in camouflage shouted as they spotted him. The FAMAS rammed back into Bolan's shoulder with the recoil of the rifle grenade. The three men did not dive for the dirt. Their weapons snarled on full-auto as they charged, screaming with suicidal fury.

The grenade detonated among them. The man in the

rear lost his rifle and flailed as metal fragments ripped him apart. The other two came on. Bolan fired quick bursts from his weapon. The remaining two Javanese staggered forward, taking hit after hit. One finally went down bleeding from a dozen wounds. The other screamed incoherently before finally dropping.

Bolan's rifle clacked open on a smoking, empty chamber. He ejected the spent magazine and reached for a fresh one.

Babar came charging out of the trees.

The giant African loped forward. He held his rifle low and smiled at Bolan over the point of his fixed bayonet.

The Executioner swung his rifle down to block, but exhaustion had robbed him of his speed. The plastic furniture of their weapons clacked, but Bolan barely managed a deflection. The blade slid away from his centerline and rammed into his side. Bolan's breath exploded from his lungs as he was slammed backward and pinned against the tree trunk.

Babar grunted with effort as the bayonet point caught in the woven fibers of Bolan's battered armor. The Executioner's left hand wrapped around Babar's throat, but his broken fingers could exert no leverage to choke him and he did not have the strength to hold off the giant Senegalese. Babar put all of his weight behind his rifle and drove the bayonet home. The point punched through Bolan's armor and steel burned into his side. The knife's edge skidded along one of his ribs and the point punched out the back of his vest. Babar grinned in savage triumph and ripped the bloody blade free for the killing thrust.

Bolan's right hand came up with the silenced Beretta

pistol from his belt, and he shot Babar three times in the face.

The giant slowly toppled to the floor of the jungle with a thud. Bolan sagged forward and nearly fell on top of him. He pushed himself to his knees and painfully stripped off his defeated body armor. The wound along his ribs was long and ragged, but shallow. But it was one more wound about to go septic, and in the killing heat of the jungle Bolan just couldn't spare any more of his blood.

He grabbed Babar's canteen and drank it dry.

Slightly refreshed, he took Babar's medical kit and bound and rebound his wounds. His entire rib cage was wrapped like a mummy. Bolan pulled on the ragged remnants of his shirt and stripped the dead legionnaire of his undamaged rifle, spare magazines and rifle grenades. He wolfed down the Swiss chocolate from Babar's ration pack for quick energy and stood with a groan. He went and took the canteens from the fallen Javanese. Two were perforated and leaking, and he drank their contents before the floor of the jungle could. One was intact and half full, and he clipped it to his belt.

Bolan turned toward the river and wearily began walking.

Islamov and Knock-Knock remained. They would be waiting for him by the river.

Bolan dropped low and crept through the jungle. He ignored the wounds in his sides as he slithered from cover to cover. He inched forward toward the sound of the river and stopped when he could smell it.

Bolan strained his senses for signs of the enemy. Only the burbling of the river against its banks came back. He moved forward until he could see the brown water moving swiftly. It was about forty yards across. The jungle made a solid wall on either side of it. Bolan moved to the water's edge and waited. He glanced at his watch and drank a little more water from his canteen. Waiting went to the enemy's advantage. Time was running out. The river was his only option.

The enemy was waiting for him to do it.

Bolan emptied his pack of all nonessentials. Swimming the river with two rifles was an ugly enough proposition. He grabbed the exposed roots of a tree and slowly lowered himself into the water. He waited among the reeds with his eyes and nose barely above the water. A few stray thoughts of open wounds and piranhas entered his mind, but he didn't have the time to entertain them. He took long, slow breaths to oxygenate his lungs.

Bolan sank beneath the surface and kicked off.

The brown water was opaque except for the top two feet where the sun shone down directly upon the surface. Bolan stayed down in the deeper, darker water and let the current take him. He frog-kicked lazily, letting the river do his work for him. He ignored his lungs as they began to revolt against the lack of oxygen in his blood. He kicked on calmly until his vision began to darken and color, and then smoothly broke for the surface.

Bolan sucked air even as he heard the shout behind him and the thump of the grenade launcher. He sank to the bottom. A moment later the surface of the river pulsed orange. The shock wave pressed Bolan's eardrums like stabbing screwdrivers. He pushed back up and broached the surface, kicking his legs to stay afloat and firing his FAMAS back at the figure of Islamov a hundred yards away by the bank.

Islamov ripped off a burst, and the water a few feet from Bolan chopped with bullet strikes. The Executioner's grenade flew wide, but Islamov ducked back into the trees as the grenade detonated on the bank. He sank beneath the surface again. He had to do distance or stay a sitting duck every time he surfaced. Bolan opened his hands and let the FAMAS slide from his fingertips and slip down into the darkness. He reached out and swam. The wounds in his sides pulled and reopened as Bolan reached out and opened his stroke. There was a bend in the river fifty yards ahead. From there he could get out of the line of sight and consider his options.

Bolan swam and surfaced.

Twice bullets sought him as he breached and sucked air. The third time he came up he had put the bend between himself and Islamov. Bolan surfaced exhaustedly and breaststroked slowly with the current. He couldn't swim much longer. The rifle slung across his back was a lead weight, and he simply didn't have it in him. Bolan slowed and trod water. He turned his head to glance back as he heard noise behind him.

Knock-Knock was in the water and around the bend.

The Vietnamese had removed his boots and shirt, and abandoned his rifle. He switched from a powerful crawl to a smooth breaststroke that kept his head out of the water as he stroked toward Bolan.

The legionnaire held his bayonet in his teeth.

Bolan drew the Beretta. He nearly slid under the surface as he tried to tread water with just his legs and one exhausted arm. The Beretta coughed twice and water sluiced with bullet strikes a yard wide from Knock-Knock's head. The legionnaire's face was a grimace around the blade as he came on. Bolan tried to steady himself for another shot but sank. His shot went into the air as the water closed over his head. Bolan strangled as he breathed river. His wounds tore as his lungs convulsed. He lost his pistol as he gagged and clawed to get himself above water.

Bolan hacked water from his lungs and flailed to stay afloat. Knock-Knock swam on easily, letting the river do his work as he closed in. He did not blink as he watched Bolan's struggles. The Executioner reached down to his belt. He almost sank again as he drew his bayonet. He put the blade between his teeth and alternately coughed out water and sucked in air around the bitter metal as he waited for Knock-Knock.

Islamov's voice boomed from around the bend in the river. "Knock-Knock!"

Knock-Knock stopped a few yards from Bolan and took the knife from his mouth. "A few more moments, Commander!" His eyes never left Bolan's as he shouted back. "A few moments!"

Bolan stopped treading water. He spit out his blade and sank.

He could hear Knock-Knock diving after him. Bolan desperately unslung the four-foot rifle as he went down. The legionnaire appeared as a dark shape in the brown light above. Bolan's finger closed around the trigger of the rifle.

Knock-Knock seized the weapon by the stock and shoved. He had let go of his own blade, as well. He and Bolan struggled with the rifle barred between them. Knock-Knock pushed down relentlessly, forcing Bolan deeper into the brown gloom. The legion commando was at the peak of physical fitness, and still relatively fresh. Bolan was wounded and exhausted.

All Knock-Knock had to do was hold Bolan down in the dark waters until he died.

Bolan blew out the air in his straining lungs and went with the steady downward pressure. Bolan's wounds screamed as he took a momentary respite from the struggle and pulled his knees into his chest. He put his boots into Knock-Knock and then straightened his body with every ounce of might he had left.

The rifle ripped free from Knock-Knock's hands.

The back of Bolan's head and shoulders scraped the river bottom. Bolan coiled to get his feet under him and exploded upward, thrusting the rifle ahead of him like a spear. The muzzle thudded into something hard and Bolan squeezed the trigger. The weapon twisted in his hands with recoil, and the sound of the high power rifle going off underwater was like a bomb.

Bolan clawed his way upward for air. His sodden boots gave him no leverage in the water. There was nothing left in his lungs. His life bled out of his sides. Bolan's vision narrowed into a dark tunnel lit with tiny purple pinpricks of light. His struggle became less intense as his limbs slowed. A strange peace calmed Bolan's mind. The strain in his lungs eased as he began to die.

The Executioner's lungs exploded in a ragged gasp for life as he broke the surface. He dog-paddled feebly and wheezed. By some unconscious instinct, he had retained the rifle.

Knock-Knock bobbed to the surface and floated past Bolan with the current. He lay facedown in the water, and his blood mixed with the brown water around him. Bolan heard splashes from the shore. The gunshots and grenade strikes in the water had driven off the caimans and the piranhas. The smell of blood was swiftly bringing them back. Knock-Knock was bleeding a river. Bolan himself was leaking like a sieve.

The Executioner groaned with effort and began swimming for the opposite shore.

17

The sun was setting. Beneath the multitiered canopy of the rain forest the darkness of the jungle floor was already growing thick. The birds had settled into their nests for the night. Bats rose up on leathery wings to feast on the insects that were already rising in swarms and eating Bolan alive. Other predators would be rising to stalk the darkness. The jungle was mostly impenetrable by day, and there were no stars in the jungle canopy to guide at night.

Bolan was fairly certain a town was somewhere to the west. He had hoped to find signs of it, or at least the next river, before the sun fell. He drank the last of his water and ate aspirins from the medical kit. The wounds in his side were hot, and he was waiting for the beginnings of fever.

Bolan raised his head and sniffed the air.

He was either already hallucinating or he smelled coffee. He unshouldered his rifle and began walking toward the smell. He was fairly sure that Islamov would not try to entice him to his doom by brewing up late-night frappucinos in the middle of the jungle, but that didn't mean the legionnaire wasn't close and could smell it, too. Soon Bolan smelled cigarettes. He could see the orange glow of a campfire through breaks in the trees.

The soldier squatted outside the light of the fire and observed the campers.

A black man and an Indian sat on a log in front of the fire. Beyond them the jungle opened up onto a small strip of beach. The long, skinny canoe was dragged up on the sand. The river gleamed in the last rays of the sun beyond. Coffee brewed in a cast iron frying pan set on two hoops of metal over the fire. The Indio was expertly cleaning a fish. The Creole was cleaning lengths of wire with a rag. A double-barreled shotgun rested across his knees.

Bolan eyed the ocelot and jaguar pelts stretched across homemade drying racks and knew the two men's business.

The Executioner stepped into the camp.

The two men froze. The Creole's hands lowered an inch toward his shotgun and stopped as he saw the high-powered rifle in Bolan's hands. He cleared his throat. "Good evening."

Bolan glanced at the Indio and his fish. "You having piranha?"

The Indio's knife stayed frozen in his hand as he nodded slowly.

The Creole eyed Bolan's shredded, soaked and bloodstained clothing. "It looks like the piranha had you."

"They tried." Bolan smiled wearily. "So did the caimans. So did the legion."

Bolan knew he played the right card as the two men sat up straighter. Poaching was good in the area, but that was because most men poaching protected animals did not want to run into foreign legion jungle warfare patrols. Being beaten, robbed, bound and left for the authorities was probably the best they could hope for. The Indio lowered his fish and his knife. "They are operating in the area?"

Bolan pointed back the way he had come. "East, on the other side of the last river."

The poachers glanced at each other and did mental calculations. They looked back at Bolan and his scope-sighted rifle.

"Where's the nearest town?" Bolan asked.

The Indio lifted his jaw toward the river. "Saul is nearest. About thirty kilometers, up river."

"You'd better go," Bolan said.

The two men nodded and then froze as Bolan reached into his pocket. They leaned forward again as Bolan produced a somewhat abused and waterlogged money clip. Despite its battered state, the poachers could not help but appreciate how thick it was.

"I'll pay you a lot of money to take me with you."

BOLAN FED more coins into the pay phone. French Guiana did not have the most technologically sophisticated telephone exchange, but it was awfully strange for all circuits to be busy at seven o'clock in the morning.

Something was wrong.

Bolan gave the machine the last of his coins. Calling the Farm internationally from a public phone was a huge breach of security, but time was running out, and secure satellite links were few and far between in the Guianan rain forest. Bolan breathed a sigh of relief as the line began to make international beeps and chimes. A large, Creole policeman in a blue-and-white uniform slowly motored down the cobblestone lane on a very old BMW motorcycle.

The line picked up. Bolan recognized the voice of one of the secretaries who screened nonsecure calls the Farm received, and then routed them or had them traced. "Hello, how may I help you?"

"Ellie, this is Striker. I have some problems."

Ellie paused. "I'm going to need verification."

"Striker, call sign—" Bolan paused as the policeman puttered slowly by. He took in Bolan's ragged appearance as he passed. The policeman suddenly whipped his head back around as he spotted the rifle leaning in the corner of the phone booth. Bolan grimaced. There wasn't going to be time for security codes and clearance. "Contact Hal! Give him this message! Launch at Kourou must be stopped! Tell—"

The policeman spun his motorcycle in a circle. He dropped the ancient bike on its side and slapped leather. He came up with an equally ancient looking Lebel revolver. *"Arrêt!"*

Bolan froze and spoke slowly and clearly. "Tell Hal…broken arrow."

The policeman gestured with his revolver at the phone. "Stop."

"Tell Hal broken arrow. Repeat, broken arrow."

The police cocked back the hammer of his pistol.

Ellie spoke rapidly over the line. "Striker! Please confirm—"

Bolan slowly hung up the phone and put up his hands. *"Bonjour,* Officer."

The policeman cocked his head slightly. "An American?"

"Yes, I was hunting upriver. My canoe capsized."

Bolan kept his hands up but glanced down at his tattered condition and shrugged. "The piranha nearly made a meal of me. I was in the jungle for forty-eight hours. Some fisherman found me and brought me in a few minutes ago."

The policeman stared at Bolan's shredded and bloodstained garments.

"I was trying to call the United States to tell my wife I am all right, but nearly all the circuits are busy. What is happening?"

"It is a terrible thing." The policeman nodded and lowered his pistol. "The U.S. Embassy in Suriname has been bombed. I am sure the switchboards in both countries have been flooded with international calls."

Bolan's insides went cold. He had every faith that it was an attempt to deny him assets and direct U.S. Intelligence attention away from Kourou. The policeman smiled. "You say two fisherman brought you in a few minutes ago?"

Bolan nodded. "Yes, they were most helpful."

"If it was the two men I saw on the docks a few moments ago, those men are poachers and smugglers. You are very lucky to be alive." The policeman's smile turned totally professional. "I will need to see your identification."

"Certainly, Officer, I—" Bolan's left hand shot and seized the policeman's gun hand. His right thumb shot into the notch between the officer's collarbones and violently compressed his trachea. The policeman's eyes flew wide as he gagged. Bolan swung his boot up between the officer's legs. As the man folded, Bolan chopped the edge of his hand into the side of his neck.

Early in the morning there was very little moving in

the frontier jungle town of Saul save the morning fog off the river.

Bolan dragged the unconscious policeman down an alley. He stripped him, gagged him, bound him and put him in trash bin. The police uniform was a size too large as Bolan shrugged into it but it would pass casual inspection. The soldier strapped on the policeman's belt and revolver. He reclaimed his rifle and went out onto the street. Bolan picked up the ancient BMW motorcycle from the cobblestones. The bike coughed blue smoke as he kicked it back into life. It wasn't a Ducati by any stretch of the imagination, but it would have to serve.

Bolan checked his watch. The hands swept unstoppably toward the launch hour.

It was 150 miles to Kourou.

18

Kourou Space Center

"He is alive."

Thana Al-Habsi's knuckles whitened around her cell phone. "Really."

"If the jungle has not killed him—" Islamov's voice sounded exhausted "—he will be coming."

"What is the status of your team?" the woman asked.

"All dead."

"Dead?" The woman was stunned. "He killed all of you?"

"All, save myself. It took me some time to get out the jungle, and I had to avoid the Jungle Warfare camp and my fellow legionnaires."

Irar Sahad came over and leaned in close to Thana. "What is happening?"

"Islamov's team has been annihilated." Thana shook her head. "He says the American is coming."

Sahad took the phone. "Islamov, you say the American is coming. How could he possibly reach the space center in time?"

"At this point, I will put nothing past him. If he reached a town alive..." Islamov paused. "French Guiana is not such a large place, and the distance is not insurmountable."

"But what can he do?" Sahad shook his head. "He is but one man."

"That one man, wounded and exhausted, slaughtered my entire team, by himself, in the jungle." Islamov's voice went steely. "He will be coming."

Sahad's teeth clenched. He'd had had quite enough of the American, as well as Islamov's and Thana's failures to figure out who he was, much less capture or kill him. Sahad looked at the clock on the wall. Living or dead, the American was now a nonissue. "The French foreign legion is actively hunting him in connection with Commandant Marmion's death. The police are looking for him, as well, and with the bombing attack on the U.S. Embassy, the roads are swarming with soldiers and police. We have received no word of the U.S. government demanding a stop to the launch. Even if he has managed to contact his people, it will take far too long politically for anything to be done. The French government will not be pleased by demands to stop a launch because of wild American stories. Particularly if the launch involves one of their most sophisticated new observation satellites. They will find that very suspicious, far too suspicious to suspend the launch, and should inquiries be made, everything here at the space center will appear perfectly normal."

Sahad glanced at the clock again with great satisfaction. "And there is no time for any of that. So what can he do?"

"He will come."

"So he comes!" Sahad scoffed. "Security here at

Kourou has been quadrupled. What is this lone American going to do? Assault the space center by himself?"

Islamov spoke slowly and clearly over the phone, as if he were trying to explain something very important to a willful child. "The American will be coming. He will be coming to stop the launch. He will be coming for both of you."

Sahad paused as a direct threat to his life finally registered.

He lowered the phone as Feresteh Mohammedkhani came through the double doors of the lounge. She smiled. "There you are, Dr. Seth. Everyone is looking for you." She looked at her watch in excitement. "We launch within the hour. You are needed in the control room."

"Thank you, Feresteh." Sahad nodded toward Thana. "Miss Erulin wished to discuss some last-minute security measures she wishes instituted on the launch area."

Thana nodded. Sahad smiled benevolently at her. For all her brilliance, the Persian bitch suspected nothing.

Thana smiled at Mohammedkhani, as well. "You must be very excited. With Dr. Poulain in hospital, this will be your first launch command. Congratulations."

"Thank you, though I wish Dr. Poulain were here." The rocket scientist's face fell. "Have we had any word of...?"

It took Thana an effort of will to keep the smile of cruelty from her face. "No, we are looking for the site of his helicopter crash. I will let you know as soon as I learn anything."

"Thank you." Dr. Mohammedkhani looked at her watch. "We must return to the main control room, now."

Sahad nodded. "We will be with you presently."

They watched her leave, and Dr. Seth handed the phone to Thana in irritation. "Here. You talk to him."

Thana took the phone. "Come as quickly as you can."

"I am on my way." Islamov's voice dropped low. "Was that Dr. Mohammedkhani?"

Thana smiled. "Yes, she is very excited about her launch. But she is worried about her American boyfriend."

"I am worried about him, too. Once the rocket is successfully launched, kill her."

Thana's smile grew predatory. "With pleasure."

THE BMW WAS BURNING OIL. Her temperature needle was firmly locked against the post in the red, but Bolan had no time to nurse the ancient iron along. All she had to do was survive another twenty minutes. The region was in an uproar with the bombing of the U.S. Embassy. Soldiers and police were everywhere.

One policeman tearing along the road on a motorcycle raised no attention whatsoever.

A simple salute had allowed him to go around the last three roadblocks without stopping. Bolan weaved through downtown traffic. His uniform and vehicle had allowed him to burn nonstop all the way from Saul to Kourou. His uniform would not be enough to let him slide through the gates of the space center. The minute he opened his mouth his ruse would be over.

He passed a convoy of oversize half-ton trucks dripping with armed legionnaires heading for the space center. The center was only a few miles outside of town. As Bolan approached the great flat plains of the launch areas, he saw the double electric fences topped with razor wire. The roadside flanking the fences swarmed with people and parked cars. People played soccer in the open areas by the road. People ate and drank and played guitars. Everyone was constantly checking their watches and listening to the countdown on portable radios. French Guiana had a small population. Nearly everyone in the town of Kourou worked directly for the space center or supported its employees. Launchings were big events, and everyone who could turned out to watch them. Already, people were drifting away from their diversions and shading their eyes as they looked out across the launch fields.

The slender white spire of the Ariane-5 rocket gleamed in the tropical sun. The gantry had been rolled away and the rocket stood alone.

Launch was imminent.

Bolan brought his motorcycle to a halt. He couldn't bluff his way through the gate, and he would be cut to pieces in seconds if he charged it. Ramming double electrified fences on a battered BMW would be equally suicidal. He'd just have to go airborne. Bolan eyed the stately palm trees that lined the perimeter road.

There was forty-footer a hundred yards down that would do.

Bolan road his bike to the tree. Palms had stiff skins but were soft and pulpy on the inside, and quite easy to cut through. Unfortunately, he didn't have an ax. The Executioner turned as a jeep drove slowly down the road. A pair of armed legionnaires were inside inspecting the scattered crowds.

Bolan parked his bike. He smiled and waved them over.

The jeep pulled off the road. One of the legionnaires got out. He slung his rifle over his shoulder and smiled.

Bolan spun his FR-F1 sniper rifle around on its sling. The legionnaire barely had time to start in surprise as

Bolan rammed him in the midriff with the muzzle of the sniper rifle. The man wheezed and bent, and Bolan's buttstroke nearly lifted the legionnaire out of his boots.

The legionnaire in the jeep shouted and fumbled for his pistol.

Bolan closed on the vehicle in three strides. The windshield was down. He vaulted up onto the bumper and then the hood. The legionnaire just cleared leather with his Beretta when Bolan's boot swung up under his jaw like a field goal kicker. The legionnaire collapsed in his seat.

People nearby shouted and pointed at the policeman who had struck down two legionnaires.

Bolan slung the sniper rifle and took up the unconscious soldier's FAMAS assault weapon. The legionnaires were patrolling a military launch, and there had been vague threats of an attack. They were armed with rifle grenades. Bolan chose a blue, antiarmor munition and clicked it over the muzzle.

People began pointing and shouting at Bolan in earnest.

The Executioner walked up to the palm tree, took a rough estimate at how it would most likely fall and fired at its base.

The FAMAS rammed back in recoil. The grenade's shaped charge payload detonated and the jet of superheated gas and molten metal sheared through the base of the palm. People began screaming. The palm shuddered as its base was cut from under it, and Bolan ran for the BMW as the tree began to topple.

A mixed group of launch watchers began clustering into an outraged mob.

Bolan held the FAMAS rifle's trigger on full-auto and sprayed an entire magazine over the crowd's heads.

People scattered screaming in all directions. Bolan tossed away the spent assault weapon and kicked the BMW into life.

The palm let out a groan as it slowly fell across the road. Metal tore and sparks screamed as it crashed into the fence. Sap sizzled and the smell of charring pulp filled the air. The first fence had nearly collapsed, but the second had held the weight of the tree. The palm hung suspended at a fifty-degree angle. People were running every which way. Alarms began to ring on loudspeakers across the launch fields.

Down the road, the convoy of legionnaire trucks came into view.

Bolan took the BMW down the road a bit and then turned in a tight circle. He took an oblique angle at the trunk and popped a wheelie as he accelerated. The rear wheel ground against the trunk, and Bolan turned the front tire to fall across it. The bike skidded and the soldier nearly dropped it as it wobbled. The rear wheel bit and Bolan was on the trunk. He twisted his wrist back and sent the bike shooting along the trunk full throttle. The palm began to bow with the weight as Bolan picked up speed.

The giant fan of leaves at the top of the tree had begun to burn. Bolan held the throttle down and the ancient engine screamed into the red line. He and the bike punched through the curtain of flaming palm fronds.

His stomach dropped as he and the bike went airborne.

Launch Control Bunker One

"TEN MINUTES and counting." The young launch control engineer's voice grew giddier with each passing minute he announced.

Sahad stared at the boards. All systems were go. His triumph was total. He stared out at the Ariane-5 with palpable anticipation. The rocket's payload was the sum total of his life's effort. Everything had been designed according to specifications. The orbital thrusters, the solar wings, the size, the shape, the weight, everything down to the last detail. Only there was no highly sensitive observation suite. The high-powered thermal imaging equipment, the ultra-sensitive radars, the highly sophisticated computers and powerpacks that serviced them had been omitted. No one save Sahad and his team knew this. They ran all the tests. They reported that everything was functioning perfectly. Outwardly, the satellite met all weight and design specifications.

Only Sahad and his team knew that in the belly of the satellite lay a thermonuclear weapon, sheathed in powdered cobalt.

The satellite would ascend into space in exactly the planned trajectory and assume its assigned orbit. However, when it passed over the United States it would deviate from orbit. It would fold its solar wings, fire its thrusters, and reenter Earth's atmosphere. Nothing would guide it from that point. It would be a simple ballistic trajectory. The satellite would plunge to Earth. Sahad and his team felt they could predict with accuracy that it would hit somewhere within a one-hundred-kilometer radius of the target point. The target point had been adjusted a hundred kilometers east of the ocean to make sure of an overland detonation.

Low altitude burst had been chosen so that the half-megaton explosion would draw up the maximum amount of dust and debris into the fireball. That dust and debris would become radioactive fallout. At the same time it would mix with the eight tons of powdered cobalt sheathing the weapon.

The fireball would imbue the cobalt with radioactivity, but by its nature, cobalt emitted absorbed radiation in a vastly more rapid and violent fashion than most other elements. Every particle of cobalt would spew forth its absorbed radioactivity like a fiercely burning sun. In a matter of hours, every living thing within two hundred miles would have received a lethal dose of radiation.

This of course, would be in addition to the heat and blast effects of the half-megaton explosion, and, over the course of time, the slower, more insidious radioactivity of the normal, persistent fallout of the regular dust and debris.

Sahad's smile was beatific.

America's darkest day was only a matter of hours away.

Designing, building and substituting the weapon had been the easiest part of the plan. It had taken ten years for Irar Sahad to assume the identity of Babu Seth. Ten years earlier, two promising aerospace engineers had died. To the world at large, Irar Sahad had died in a car crash in Karachi. Babu Seth had been strangled while on vacation in Goa. Seth's immediate family died almost simultaneously in a terrible fire, and Irar had taken his place, taking his scholarship to study aerospace technology in France.

No one in Paris had known that the promising young Hindu scientist from Goa was really a highly motivated Muslim from Kashmir. He graduated with honors and did everything in his power to enhance the French space program. His mission had been vague. Perhaps the opportunity to blow up or destroy a U.S.-European joint space station, or to put a weapon in a satellite being taken into space by a U.S. space shuttle.

Then when this project had begun, Sahad had felt the glowing glory of inspiration. His plan had been enthusiastically approved, and Sahad had put it into motion.

Other sleeper agents, such as Thana in the Action Direct had gotten themselves transferred to French Guiana. The French foreign legion in Guiana was in charge of security at Kourou, and the Muslims among them had been converted to the cause and recruited. They had seen that others were recruited and transferred.

"Five minutes and counting." The launch control technician could no longer control his enthusiasm as he looked up from his boards. "She's a beauty, Dr. Seth."

"Yes, Remi." Sahad smiled benevolently. "She is—"

Alarms began to shrill in the control room.

"Remi! What is happening?"

"I don't know!" Every engineer and technician was scanning their boards feverishly. All read everything was perfect with the rocket.

"Those are the security alarms." Thana drew her pistol. "The perimeter has been breached."

Dr. Mohammedkhani was staring, dumbstruck, out the massively reinforced observation window. "There is a policeman on launch field one. On a motorcycle." She picked up a pair of binoculars from the counter. "He has a rifle." She lowered the binoculars in shock as they revealed the man's face. "It is—"

"Emergency launch!" Sahad's voice rose to a hysterical pitch. "Launch now!"

BOLAN TORE across the launch field. The legionnaires charging in pursuit did not worry him. The wheeled armored personnel carriers rolling out of the building complex and their 20 mm automatic cannons did. Bolan kept his eyes on his target as the alarms continued to clang and howl throughout the space center. The Ariane-5 was massive, and all Bolan had was a .30-caliber rifle with six rounds remaining in the magazine.

He had two things working in his favor.

Like all modern rockets, the Ariane-5 was made of aluminum, and aluminum as absolutely thin as the designers thought they could get away with. Save for some internal bracings, the rocket was a big aluminum balloon, and far from bulletproof.

And that gigantic aluminum balloon was filled with more than a hundred tons of highly volatile chemical fuel.

Bolan heard gunshots and tried to ignore them as he drove toward the control bunker. The bunker was a low, gracefully swept arc of concrete made to survive any rocket mishap. It was the only place on the field that offered any cover from the weapons that sought him.

The French gunners were trying to track his speeding motorcycle, but the range was closing by the second, and there could be up to ten heavily armed legionnaires inside.

The bunker was the only place that would give Bolan any chance at all of surviving what he was about to attempt.

Another cannon joined the first, and Bolan flinched as the shell's sonic booms cracked over his head one on top of the other in automatic fire. Bolan pulled the bike around the front of the bunker. Concrete ripped and shattered across the top as the structure temporarily sheltered Bolan. He dropped the bike and unslung his rifle. He glanced back at one of the bunker's observation slits. Through the massively thick ballistic glass Bolan could see Mohammedkhani among a crowd of scientists staring at him.

Bolan raised his rifle as he turned back to the task at hand.

The soldier was not a chemical engineer, but he had been around rockets before. In their liquid states, the two fuel elements were stable, and it took the active effort of the rocket engine's igniters and pumps to channel them, mix them and ignite them into propulsive fuel. But to keep them in the liquid state, the two elements had to be kept in sealed, separate chambers. If those chambers were breached in any way, the liquid oxygen and liquid hydrogen would begin boiling off into their gaseous state.

They would then become highly volatile. Even more so when mixed.

Bolan put the crosshairs of the FR-F1's telescopic sight on the upper stage engine. He ignored the alarms and the sound of approaching vehicles as he scanned the top of the upper-stage and found the boil-off valve. The air shimmered around the valve with little ice flakes as the invisible, supercold hydrogen mixed with vapors in the air. Bolan lowered his sight. The boil-off valve for the liquid oxygen was much easier to detect as it intermittently spewed out white clouds of uncongealing oxygen.

The hydrogen was on top. The oxygen was on the bottom. Bolan needed both of them boiling off, and a spark.

Bolan raised his rifle and fired. His bullet struck the

side of the upper-stage a few feet from where he judged the centerline to be. Nothing appeared to happen, and he dropped his aim two yards down and flicked the bolt and fired again. Bolan was instantly rewarded with a white plume of pressurized liquid oxygen squirting out of the side of the rocket and going gaseous. He examined his first hole and was pleased to see the shimmer of the invisible, negative 412-degree Fahrenheit gas forming ice flakes as it mixed with the outside air.

The Executioner heard the thunder of helicopter blades.

He worked the bolt and fired twice more, punching two more holes a foot apart from the first two. The gasses were clearly mixing, but he was not getting a catastrophic ignition.

A helicopter swept over the bunker, and bullets sprayed past Bolan's head and smashed into the bunker. He could clearly see Islamov leaning out of the bubble canopy with a FAMAS rifle. Bolan ignored the Russian as he raised his rifle and put his crosshairs on the pilot. Bolan fired and the canopy shattered with the bullet strike. The helicopter lurched as the pilot was hit. Islamov was nearly dumped from the helicopter, and his rifle fell from his hands as he held on for dear life. He heaved himself back in the cockpit and grabbed for the loose the joystick.

Bolan swung his rifle back on the Ariane-5 and fired his last round.

Nothing happened.

Bolan dropped the spent rifle and drew the antique Lebel pistol he had taken from the policeman. He raised it in both hands and emptied it in rapid fire into the cockpit of the helicopter. The chopper banked steeply to the right and then roared off under control away from the bunker area. Bolan turned. He could hear the whining and roaring of the armored personnel carriers as they closed in on the bunker. He reloaded the revolver from the rounds on the police belt.

The soldier glanced up at a sudden rippling, sibilant hissing noise.

Pale flame jetted out of the side of the Ariane's upper-stage like a match flaring. It was joined by a second, a third and a fourth as the liquid hydrogen and oxygen ignited under high pressure. The jets grew larger and longer as the holes in the tanks ripped wider under the burning pressure. Bolan turned and ran up the sloped front of the concrete bunker.

Cannonfire ripped into life as the surprised gunners of the APCs saw Bolan jump up into their sights. Bolan ran across the roof and leaped down. The back of the bunker was a blank concrete wall save for a short, narrow stairwell that lead to a reinforced steel door.

Bolan stood locked in the cannon sights of two armored personnel carriers with nothing but a revolver in his hand.

The turrets of the two vehicles tracked down to put him in a crossfire.

The world abruptly came to an end.

Bolan threw himself down the stairwell as God clapped his hands behind him. The air shuddered with the violence of it. Tank after tank containing ton after ton of liquid fuel detonated from the upper-stage to the lower-stage and went of like a string of titanic firecrackers. Orange flame filled the world as the burning gasses roared over the bunker in a wave. Bolan curled into a ball at the bottom of the stairwell as his hair singed and his exposed skin tightened against the searing heat. Sheets of burning liquid oxygen and hydrogen flew through the air, boiled off, went gaseous and detonated like bombs. Behind Bolan's tightly shut eyes, the world was a pulsing orange and white that silhouetted the veins in his eyelids. The concussions shook Bolan's very bones and seemed to bounce his brain in his skull.

The fire expanded around the top and sides of the bunker, and Bolan's world went white with blast furnace heat.

19

The bunker shook to its foundations with the explosion. Orange and yellow fire blasted against the observation slits and lit up the control room in shuttering shades of hell. Scientists and technicians screamed as the Ariane died in an orgy of fire.

Sahad kept his feet and walked directly to his desk. He flipped open the latches of his briefcase and pulled out the brutally shortened shape of a Russian AKSU-74 submachine gun. He snapped in a 75-round drum and racked the bolt.

Remi ran up to Sahad as he clicked the folding stock into place. The young technician was so torn between terror and tears at what had happened to the Ariane that he seemed not to notice the gun. "Dr. Seth! We must—"

Remi stopped in midsentence as Sahad shouldered the weapon and pointed it at him.

"Dr. Seth…"

Flame shot from the muzzle. Sahad's burst ripped the front of Remi's lab coat to bloody shreds, and the young technician toppled over a control console. New screaming erupted within the control room at the sound of automatic rifle fire and the sight of Remi's crumpled body.

Rage filled Sahad's breast. His dreams of smiting the United States with radioactive fire died as the last bits of the Ariane burned out on the launch pad. He turned that rage against the control-room team as he began firing burst after burst into the wildly fleeing scientists.

The door in the back of the bunker and the tunnel that lead from the bunker to the main complex were the only ways out. Sahad stalked through the control room shooting anyone who moved toward either one. As he passed, he shot people cowering under their consoles. Sahad's weapon ripped on. They would die. They would all die.

Dr. Dutronc hit Sahad in a flying, blindside tackle. Sahad slammed up against a console, and the bigger man bore him over and onto the floor. He saw stars as Dutronc pumped his fist into his face again and again. Dutronc grabbed his adversary by the throat and began bouncing his skull against the floor violently.

Dutronc suddenly fell across Sahad in a limp heap. The French scientist was pulled off of Sahad instantly, and a hand grabbed him by the arm and firmly yanked him upright. Dutronc lay dead at Sahad's feet with dark hole in the back of his head. Sahad blinked as Thana raised her pistol and aimed over his shoulder. The pistol clicked, and a woman's voice screamed. The ruby-red beam of the laser sight dipped, and the scream was cut short as the pistol cycled.

Thana scooped up Sahad's weapon and thrust it back into his hands. "None escape. They all die. Then we extract and link up with Islamov."

BOLAN OPENED his eyes. The explosions stopped as quickly as they had started. He was somewhat shocked

to be alive. Bolan gasped out a breath and coughed at
the acrid chemical stench and black smoke that filled
the air. Bits of metal began raining from the sky and tin-
kling against the smoking roof of the bunker. He
yawned against the ringing in his ears. He had given
himself a 50-50 chance of surviving the explosion. A
low-order detonation of the bomb would have been
something else entirely. Bolan peered up from the stairwell. The two armored personnel carriers were
scorched black on the outside and smoking. Bolan figured he had about five seconds before the legionnaires
collected themselves and began spilling out with their
rifles.

Through the pounding in his skull, Bolan became
aware of gunfire from inside the control bunker.

The door flung open, and a bleeding man tumbled
out screaming. "They're killing everyone! They're—"

His head snapped forward, and he fell with a bullet
in the back of his skull.

Bolan dived through the door.

A man and a woman lay dead where they had tried
to flee. Dr. Babu Seth moved through the main control
room with an automatic carbine. He walked past the
chairs and desks and methodically fired short bursts
into the cowering scientists and technicians.

The range was long for the ancient, fixed sight revolver.

"Seth!" Bolan roared as he dived behind a console.

The scientist ceased his slaughter and looked about
wildly for the voice that had thundered his name. Bolan
ran crouching along a bank of computers. A monitor
cracked and exploded near his skull as a high-explosive
round hit it. He ignored it as he threw himself into a roll

and came up with the Lebel revolver in a two-handed hold.

Sahad blinked in surprise as Bolan popped up ten feet in front of him.

The Lebel barked in Bolan's hands. He put two rounds into the scientist's stomach. The man grunted and his automatic carbine fired a burst. Bolan raised his aim and fired two more rounds into his chest.

Irar Sahad staggered and his weapon strobed into the ceiling. His mouth worked as the five holes in the front of his lab coat suddenly began to stain red. Sahad dropped his weapon and fell forward.

Feresteh Mohammedkhani screamed. "Down!"

Bolan threw himself to one side. The red dot of a laser sight swept past where his head had been and a snap of orange fire cracked where the .32-caliber exploding bullet detonated against the counter.

Bolan had one round left in the Lebel. There were no more reloads. "Where is she!"

"Near the observation windows! She's—" Her voice cut off with a shriek as an exploding round tore into the computer console on the desk over her head.

Bolan leaped up into the line of fire.

Jolie Erulin was already whipping her weapon back toward him. Bolan went for a head shot, but the range was twenty yards. Erulin jerked as Bolan's round hit her high in the shoulder. She backed up a step with the impact and resumed her shooting stance.

Bolan threw himself behind cover again as exploding rounds sought him.

The Executioner was out of bullets. The reload loops on the police belt were empty. He was down to handcuffs and a nightstick. Bolan considered his knife. It was no chance at all, but Erulin had to be stopped, or at least kept occupied until the legionnaires stormed the control room and stopped her.

"Stand up." The woman's voice interrupted Bolan's thought. "Stand up or I kill her."

Mohammedkhani made a noise of pain as the double agent did something to her.

She was going to kill them both anyway, but Bolan stood. As he did, the desk he crouched under came up with him. The computer, monitor and printer on the desk crashed to the floor and shattered and sparked. The drawers fell open and files and computer disks flew everywhere. Bolan tilted the desk before him as a shield and charged, slamming the desk into Erulin like a battering ram.

She was thrown back against the window. Bolan grabbed the nightstick from his belt and cracked the turned wood across her forearm. The pistol fell to the floor as her fingers spasmed. Bolan's backhand blow struck Erulin's temple. Her eyes rolled back in her head, and she fell as if she had been shot.

Bolan knelt beside Mohammedkhani. She had taken an exploding bullet in the bicep and was bleeding badly. He ripped off the police belt and cinched the wide leather band over the wound to compress it. She moaned and brought a hand to her bleeding scalp. "You have to get out of here," she whispered.

The Executioner nodded. There was still one last task. He glanced at a dead technician a few feet away. The man was much shorter than Bolan but overweight. There were two bloody holes in the front of his lab coat.

Bolan removed the coat and pulled it over the blue

police uniform he wore. Bolan took the dead man's badge and looped it over his neck

Mohammedkhani sucked in a panicked breath.

Bolan whirled in his crouch.

"Down! Everyone down! No one move!"

Bolan palmed his knife as legionnaires stormed into the control room.

The surviving scientists all began screaming at once. Bolan cradled the wounded rocket scientist in his arms. A legionnaire with a fixed bayonet appeared over them and ran his eyes over Bolan's bloody lab coat and the woman's wounds.

Bolan identified himself. "Dutronc." He jerked his head down. "Dr. Mohammedkhani."

The legionnaire nodded sharply. "Are there any more terrorists?"

Mohammedkhani let out a groan. "I saw someone with a gun. He ran downstairs, toward the lavatory."

The legionnaire shouted above the tumult. "One more possible! The lavatories!" Legionnaires rushed to put the door in a crossfire. Others fixed rifle grenades. The legionnaire glanced down quickly. "Can you walk?"

They nodded.

The legionnaire jerked his rifle toward the back door. "Go. Get out of here!"

They joined the stream of escaping scientists and walked out of the bunker into the daylight. Thick clouds of black smoke filled the sky. The Ariane-5 had been obliterated. The launch pad and the field around it were scorched. The frame of the gantry listed on its massive rollers. Armored vehicles, army trucks, ambulances and police cars were tearing toward the bunker from every direction across the launch field. Bolan supported Mohammedkhani as they limped out onto the field. She clutched a kerchief to her scalp. Her face was pale, but her gray eyes were focused and clear.

Bolan glanced up into the black clouds obscuring the sun. "Islamov has a helicopter."

"Islamov?" Mohammedkhani blinked at him.

"Ilyanov. He was the ringleader in the legion and a wanted terrorist in Russia. His real name is Islamov."

"So he got away?"

"Not yet." Bolan stared south across the launch field toward where the solid wall of the jungle started again. "I know where he's going."

She sighed. "So you need a helicopter."

"I do."

She looked past the launch field toward the airstrip. "We have three of them here for liaison duty at any given time. You think you can steal one?"

Helicopters were already thundering across the field. One was military, one was police, and two were medical that had flown in from the capital. Stealing one would be easy. The question was would French Mirage fighter jets come screaming up at Mach 2 and blow him out of the sky ten minutes after he got airborne.

There wasn't much choice. Islamov wasn't leaving French Guiana alive. "Yeah, I can steal one."

20

Bolan banked the helicopter and took a slow orbit around the jungle resupply camp. A red helicopter like his own sat in the tiny clearing. Its bubble canopy was pocked with several of Bolan's bullet strikes. Blood smeared the canopy from within. The pilot was slumped forward in his seat. The passenger seat was empty.

There was no room in the small clearing, so Bolan set his helicopter down in the pond. The skids sank in the mud and the water, and water spilled into the cockpit as he shoved open his door. There was a chance the helicopter would not be able to take off again unless it was dug out.

That was the least of Bolan's concerns.

He slogged through the pond and went and examined Islamov's helicopter. Bolan noticed bloodstains on the copilot seat and red smears on the handle of the copilot's door. He looked around the grass and leaves and followed Islamov's footprints. Here and there were scattered drops of blood.

Islamov was wounded.

Bolan walked into the shade of the camouflage netting beneath the trees. The door to the bunker was open.

He went inside and did a quick survey. There had been an opened rifle crate the last time he had been inside the bunker with three FAMAS rifles in it. One of those rifles was now missing. A crate of ration packs had been torn open and a number of the packages were gone as well. Bolan took one of the FAMAS rifles for himself and grabbed a web belt with six loaded magazines in their pouches. He took a legion knapsack out of its packaging and loaded it with rations. He took a pair of canteens and filled them from plastic water bladders from another supply crate Islamov had opened. He walked across the bunker to the little table knowing what he would find.

The suitcase containing the euros was open and empty.

There was also blood on the little table and an opened medical kit missing its field dressings. Bolan came up out of the bunker and frowned as he looked into the nearly solid wall of jungle before him. Islamov was wounded. Bolan grimaced. So was he. The lacerations in Bolan's sides ached and burned. He figured the big Russian had about an hour's head start. He checked the topographic map he had taken from the helicopter.

Islamov would head south. Approximately eighteen miles southeast was the Camopi River. It ran southwest and would take him directly to the Brazilian border. The nearest city on the map was Talima, another 124 miles away. That was more distance than a wounded man on foot in the jungle was likely to make, but Bolan was sure there were villages across the border that were not on any map, and he was also sure Islamov knew where some of those villages were. The villagers there were more than likely to give a heavily armed man with wads of cash whatever aid and assistance he required, no questions asked.

There was no choice but to run Islamov down. Once the Russian reached the river, he would be gone.

Bolan covered the blue police uniform he had commandeered with an olive drab rain poncho and smeared his hands and face with black and green camouflage paint from another crate. He was about as prepared as he was going to get.

Bolan glanced at the map and at the compass dial in his watch to orient himself, then walked into the rain forest.

ISLAMOV WAS CLOSE, and it was obvious the big Russian also suspected that he was being followed. He was taking care to hide his tracks. Islamov was wounded, and he would not wear himself out trying to outpace Bolan. He would pick his spot, and then he would turn and fight.

It was time to end the game.

The Executioner crept through the undergrowth. The light became brighter ahead, and he came to a clearing. It was about as long as a football field but narrower. Rock replaced the jungle floor. The rock had broken and smoothed over thousands of years of flooding, but the arboreal giants could not find enough earth to take root and grass and reeds had taken had taken over. The morning mist hung over the clearing.

Islamov waited for him in the long grass. Bolan could feel it.

He could be a hundred yards away, or he could be six feet from Bolan's face. Bolan reached back into his pack and pulled out one of the four rifle grenades that came with the standard French assault load and clicked it on to the muzzle of his weapon. He would have to flush out his prey.

He would have to make the first move.

Bolan raised his rifle and fired. He aimed toward the middle of the clearing and off to the right. Before the grenade detonated, Bolan had loaded a second and fired it off to the left. He fired his third grenade near the opposite end of the clearing. Monkeys and birds shrieked and howled, but no answering fire came back. Islamov's self-control was admirable. He knew French grenades were issued in four packs. He would know exactly where his adversary was now, but he would not shoot and expose himself. If he missed, Bolan would return fire with a grenade, and all Bolan would have to be was close.

Islamov was waiting for Bolan's fourth grenade.

The Executioner gave it to him.

Bolan dived as a burst of rifle fire tore through the branches around him. It came from close to where the fourth grenade had detonated. He rolled up to one knee and fired a burst that ripped through the long grass and rolled again. A burst answered back and Bolan smiled to himself. He had gambled correctly. Islamov had not equipped himself with rifle grenades. The big Russian had not expected to be followed. He was on foot, alone in the jungle, and had to make sacrifices on how much weight he could carry. Food and water would be his main concern.

And all those euros took up a lot of room.

Bolan crept forward with infinite slowness. Both men were veterans of the jungle. Each knew that one false step could kill, and the slightest sound would betray. Bolan crept, froze and listened. A few yards away the Russian was doing the same. Each was waiting for the other to make a fatal mistake.

Both men froze. Rotor blades beat the air. Bolan pressed himself down, but he knew his place in the grass was perfectly visible from above. A troop transport in French army colors thundered over the clearing followed by a second. The two helicopters quickly separated. They began a slow, counterclockwise orbit around the open wound in the jungle. The French foreign legion door gunners leaned out of the helicopters on their chicken straps. The muzzles of their machine guns trained on the two hunters.

The helicopters slowed and dropped to a few feet above the grass. A squad of legionnaires leaped out of each aircraft and deployed toward Bolan and Islamov. There was nowhere to run and nowhere to hide. Bolan slowly stood. Islamov stood ten yards away. He had already thrown down his rifle. The Executioner tossed away his rifle and decided to wait to see how the cards fell. The legionnaires surrounded them. Their faces were grim masks of stone.

Bolan recognized Doherty. The look on the Irishman's face told Bolan he was about to be dealt a very crappy hand.

Bolan looked over at Islamov. He wore civilian clothing. He looked like an ecotourist save for the military web gear he wore over it. His right thigh was bandaged where one of Bolan's revolver rounds had hit him. The wound had bled through the bandaging and then dried. There were fresh wounds on his left arm and face where some shrapnel had torn him. The Russian reeled exhaustedly on his feet. He still managed to grin at Doherty.

"Hey, Mikey."

Doherty's face remained an iron mask as he regarded Valentjin Islamov. He nodded almost imperceptibly. "You are out of uniform."

"Hey." Islamov struggled to remain standing. "How about a head start? What do you say?"

"You've already had one."

"Oh? Give me another one anyway. For old times' sake." The Russian leveled his blue-eyed gaze. "I taught you everything you know. You owe me, and besides, look at me." Islamov spread his hands. He looked like death warmed over. "The jungle will finish me off in another day."

"They'd just send another team." The Irishman's face stayed stone. "The legion would hunt you to the ends of the earth."

"So?" Islamov shrugged. "What do you care?"

Anger kindled behind Doherty's eyes. "You murdered Marmion."

Islamov did not bother to deny it.

Doherty's voice lost all emotion. "You betrayed the legion."

Islamov stared into space.

Doherty took a long breath. It was true. The Russian was committed to his cause. He was willing to die for it. He regretted nothing.

Doherty looked over at Bolan. "Marmion respected and you, and despite my personal feelings, so do I."

Bolan accepted that. "How did you find us?"

"Dr. Mohammedkhani contacted me. She told us how you suspected Islamov would go to the jungle resupply camp. She said you were wounded." He shrugged. "She thought you might need help. From that location, your only logical path was fairly easy to determine."

Bolan let out a long breath. The road to hell was paved with good intentions.

Doherty squared his shoulders. "You have destroyed an Ariane rocket, compromised the space center's security, and that of Action Direct. I personally believe that you had your reasons, and acted in the interests of the United States and France. But you have created quite an ugly mess for France. We have orders from Paris to clean that mess up. Including all loose ends." Doherty genuinely looked sorry. "Our orders are quite explicit."

Bolan considered the bayonet clipped to his web belt and the twelve automatic rifles covering him.

Islamov's eyes rolled back in his head with exhaustion. He fell to his hands and knees gasping. The rifles covering Bolan rose to hold him in place. Doherty spoke bitterly. "Get up. You stand up and we'll finish it here, quick. If not we take you back, you are interrogated the hard way and then the firing squad."

Islamov grunted with effort and pushed himself up to his knees. As he did, the pin of the NATO standard fragmentation grenade fell to the grass. Only Islamov's little finger held the spring-loaded safety lever in place. Islamov's bloodshot eyes were smiling. "Fuck you, Mikey."

Doherty regarded the grenade fatalistically. "You aren't going anywhere."

"Then none of us are."

It didn't take a genius to look in Islamov's eyes and know he was perfectly willing to die.

"This isn't about France," Bolan said. "This is legion business."

"Yes." Doherty did not take his eyes off of Islamov and the grenade in his hand. "And?"

"And he and I have unfinished business."

Every legionnaire present was a corporal or a sergeant. There were no French officers present save perhaps for the helicopter pilots, and they knew to stay out of it. The honor of the legion was iron, and legion took care of its own.

This was not going to go to court martial in Paris.

Doherty came to a decision. He very slowly ejected the magazine from his rifle and emptied the round in the chamber. He tossed the empty rifle into the mud in front of Islamov. "Kill the American, and I'll give you twenty-four hours—for old times' sake."

Islamov stared long into his comrade's eyes, and an understanding passed between the two legionnaires. Islamov slowly picked up the pin from the mud and slid it back into the grenade. He lobbed the grenade over his shoulder, and the legionnaire behind him caught it. Islamov took up the fallen rifle. His bayonet rasped from the sheath on his belt, and he clicked it onto the muzzle of his rifle.

Doherty drew his Beretta pistol and backed away. He jerked his head at a legionnaire standing near Bolan.

The legionnaire ejected the magazine from his rifle and racked out the round in the chamber. He walked over to Bolan and held out the weapon.

Bolan stripped off his poncho and stood in the torn and bloodstained French police uniform. The bayonet on his hip rang free, and he fixed it to the rifle.

Doherty shook his head bitterly as he turned to

Bolan. "Finish it, and I will give you twenty-four hours, out of professional courtesy."

An Asian Bolan did not recognize barked out a command in French. "Legionnaires! Fix bayonets!"

Twenty-two blades rang from their sheaths, and the French foreign legion fixed their bayonets to their loaded rifles. No other order was given. None was needed. The situation was understood by all. It was a matter of honor. The legionnaires fanned out and formed a wide circle around Bolan and Islamov.

As Islamov came to his feet he flicked his right foot. The toe of his boot scooped up mud from the ground and flung it toward Bolan's eyes. The Executioner jerked his head aside and brought up his rifle as Islamov lunged. The Russian was nowhere near as exhausted as he pretended. He punched his bayonet toward his opponent's guts. Bolan brought his rifle before him and Islamov instantly ripped up at Bolan's face. The tip of the blade clipped Bolan's chin and blood flew. The back edge of Islamov's blade chopped back down at the side of the Bolan's neck. The soldier staggered back and brought his rifle between them. Islamov's bayonet scored the plastic stock of Bolan's rifle and came a hairbreadth from slicing off his two broken fingers.

The legionnaires watched in stony silence, ready to shoot either man if he fled the fight or tried to load his rifle from the magazines on his belt.

This was an execution.

Bolan spun the rifle around in his hand. He abandoned bayonet tactics and raised the rifle overhead like a club. Islamov's eyes widened as Bolan swung the rifle like a sledgehammer. Islamov brought up his weapon to block, and the two rifles slammed together with bone-jarring force. Islamov's wounded leg buckled as he staggered from the blow. Bolan ignored the jarring ache in his arms and arced his weapon at the Russian again like an ax. All Islamov could do was use his rifle to block the blow. The cheekpiece and buttplate of Bolan's weapon shattered off his rifle with the impact. Islamov was shoved sideways and dropped to one knee.

Bolan's bayonet was still fixed. He raised his cracked rifle overhead and then suddenly shortened his swing into a sharp downward thrust. The point of the bayonet plunged for Islamov's throat like an ice pick.

Islamov managed to get his rifle in the way. Bolan's blade grated against the carrying handle of his adversary's gun. They struggled, and Islamov surged upward and rammed his rifle at Bolan with both hands. The soldier saw stars as the handguard punched him between the eyes.

Bolan blinked blood out of his eyes as he tottered backward. Screws and springs fell out of his broken weapon and pieces of the stock shifted under his hands where they had torn loose from their moorings. Only Islamov's wounded leg kept him from leaping in and finishing it. The legionnaires stood like statues and waited for the inevitable end. Islamov took a ragged breath and raised his bayonet again. The Russian limped forward for the kill.

Bolan raised his shattered rifle and threw it.

The eight-pound weapon revolved once and slammed into both of Islamov's shins. The Russian groaned as his legs buckled, and he fell to his knees. Bolan ripped his web belt from his waist. The canvas burned between his fingers as he stripped the four magazine pouches along the belt so that they all bunched at one end.

Bolan whirled the belt around his head as Islamov rose.

The seven loaded magazines at the end of the belt blurred in an ugly arc, and six and a half pounds of brass, steel and lead collided with Islamov's skull. Bullets and springs flew as the magazines ruptured their contents. Islamov reeled. Bolan strode forward bunching the belt in his hands. The Russian half-blindly thrust his bayonet forward to hold him off. Bolan kicked it aside with the flat of his boot and looped the belt around his adversary's neck.

Islamov's gasp was cut short as Bolan crossed his hands and cinched the Russian's throat shut. Bolan rammed his hip and shoulder against Islamov's, jamming the Russian's rifle between them and smothering any attempted thrust. Islamov abandoned his rifle. Bolan's vision went white as the big Russian buried his fist into the wound in his side. Islamov's face was purpling but Bolan's sight blackened as Islamov's fist slammed into his side a second time.

The Executioner's wounds burned as he torqued his torso savagely. He dropped to one knee as he and Islamov went back to back. Bolan heaved on the belt with all of his strength. Islamov flew over Bolan's shoulder. As he flew, Bolan yanked back on the belt.

Islamov's neck snapped as he hit grass.

Bolan fell forward onto his hands and concentrated on the act of breathing as colors swam before his eyes.

The only sound was the slow threshing of the helicopter blades as their engines idled. Bolan waited for his vision to clear and then pushed himself up. He looked at the legionnaires with as much impassiveness as he could muster. They stood with their bayonets fixed and their rifles pointed. Doherty went and knelt over Islamov. He reached down and pulled the dog tags from under his shirt. The box chain broke as Doherty snapped them away. The Irishman rose and stared at Bolan long and hard. He stared down once more at Islamov's motionless corpse.

The legionnaires turned without a word. They broke into their squads and began filing back to their respective helicopters. Doherty stopped and turned. He unhooked his canteen from his belt and tossed it to Bolan.

Bolan watched the helicopters disappear across the jungle. Both wounds in his sides were bleeding. He idly wished Doherty had left him a few units of blood. Water and rations were all he was likely to get anytime soon. He listened to the thunder of the rotors fade into the distance. Action Direct wanted him dead, and the French foreign legion had orders to kill. Bolan glanced around at the jungle surrounding him. He had been given an ugly reprieve.

He had twenty-four hours to get out of French Guiana.

Bolan noticed Islamov's pack in the grass. He walked over and examined the contents, keeping what was useful and ejecting wasted weight.

He took enough euros to get him where he needed to go.

The rest of the money ended up in the mud.

Bolan drank some water. He checked the compass in his watch and took out his map again. It was midsummer. The equatorial sun was rising toward noon. It was 125 miles to Brazil.

Bolan began walking south.

James Axler
Outlanders®

EVIL ABYSS

An ancient kingdom harbors awesome secrets...

In the heart of Cambodia, a portal to the eternal mysteries of space and time lures both good and evil to its promise. Now, a deadly imbalance has not only brought havoc to the region, but it also threatens the efforts of the Cerberus warriors. To have control of the secrets locked deep within the sacred city is to possess the power to manipulate earth's vast energies...and in the wrong hands, to alter the past, present and future in unfathomable ways....

Available February 2005 at your favorite retail outlet.

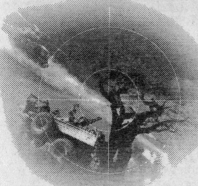

THE DESTROYER

DREAM THING

DEMONIC GOD—OR FISH STORY?

A strange seismic disturbance in the south Pacific has put the world in a fighting mood. Violence is especially high among the peaceniks, as spiritualists morph into savage mobs. Scientists acknowledge that the oceans are shrinking, but nobody can explain why.

Steam vents as big as volcanoes burst open around the world. But is it free geothermal power...or a death knell? A typhoon smashes Hawaii; the Amazon is a killer sauna; Rocky Mountain skiers are steamed like clams. Is the world succumbing to a theoretical Tectonic Hollow...or the will of a giant squid? Either way, it just won a date with Remo, who's ready to fry some calamari.

Available April 2005 at your favorite retail outlet.